The Kir
K

by

JR Vost

Cover design by Barney Vost

OPTIMISM

Chapter

1

Order! Order! Order! - bellowed the speaker of the house.

Pandemonium prevailed at PMQs (Prime Minister's Questions) as the PM was taunted by the opposition over the UK's foreign policy - what foreign policy? That had, in effect, been handed over to Brussels - we no longer had a foreign policy - or any other policies come to that. Successive governments had aided and abetted the EU in emasculating the UK since Margaret Thatcher's period in office.

There was a palpable air of panic in Downing Street. It wasn't a question of if, but when there was going to be a terrorist attack on the UK mainland.

It was entirely predictable to just about everyone, except the government, that ISIL (Islamic State in Iraq and Levant) would retaliate against the air strikes we and the Americans were carrying out against them in Northern Iraq, even though they were ineffective - a few personnel and four-by-four vehicles removed, but at what cost?

The government was dreading a repeat of the Lee Rigby killing in public, or more recently the awful events in Paris and Brussels. Regardless of the state of the opposition repetition of these events in the UK would ruin any chances of re-election.

The terrorist threat level to the UK had been raised too Critical from Severe following a JIC (Joint Intelligence Committee) meeting - they were acting on information received from GCHQ (Government Communications Headquarters) - an attack was imminent. All leave for the police and security services was cancelled and the military were put on guard at all sensitive sites including airports and railway stations.

These sites had been identified many years ago, at the height of the Cold War and the troubles in Ireland, and were regularly updated.

At the same meeting a proposed change of tactics was discussed. Although each case was and will remain judged on its merits the tactics used to date were far too long-winded under the present circumstances. Because of the thoroughness of each investigation it gave suspects time to develop their particular project, take on new recruits or even disappear.

The authorities would now move more hastily in an attempt to disrupt projects at an early stage - put pressure on the plotters. The risk of course was that insufficient evidence will be collected to ensure a successful prosecution, but in the present climate that was considered to be a risk worth taking.

ISIL had designs on Iraq as the country to establish their kalifate and there was no-one to stop them. Both the UK and the USA had emphatically ruled out 'boots on the ground' - there was no appetite and with elections in a few months in America, it would be politically suicidal to invade Iraq again. NATO and the EU were dithering as usual and completely ineffectual. Yes, the French were doing their habitual muttering and posturing but to no end - there was no-one to take on ISIL. They controlled Mosul and soon they would take Baghdad, then they would have a modern, well equipped army and air force - they would be embraced by the Iraqi Sunnis after years of murder and oppression by the Shia majority - time for bloody revenge. The prognosis was grim.

Chapter

2

There was a growing crowd, or congregation outside the Mosque in North London gathering for Friday Prayers (Bahaqi), the most important of the week: it was just before 11 o'clock on a fine, warm Spring day. A rare moment of near silence in the capital, no sirens - the only sound of note was the shrill call of a Robin perched on a railing, presumably looking for a mate. Variously attired some of the assembly were wearing kaftans; among those present there were five young men in their thirties, well dressed, two of them wearing suits - all clean shaven and their black hair cut short - they looked professional, perhaps city types.

The crowd entering the Mosque was welcomed by the Imam - behind his left shoulder stood another man. The five young men, all known to this other man were directed to an annexe of the Mosque. Prayers began and after the third (Asr), another individual of similar age and attire joined the small group.

Once everyone was seated the man known to the group as Ghazal, or in English - Gazelle was ready to address them. He had met each of the group but they didn't know each other. It had taken him over year to assemble these recruits to the cause. The sixth recruit, the last to arrive, was the only one born out of the UK, he came from Iraq.

Gazelle was older than the others, very handsome and in his late-forties or early fifties, again well groomed like the group. He had typical Arab facial features and colouring, but was unusually tall. Strikingly he had wide set blue eyes and curly golden hair - a half-caste, or perhaps from Aleppo. His bearing was one of authority, evidently an important individual in Arab circles - a Sheikh maybe. Wearing an ivory colour linen suit and open neck expensively cut shirt, set off with Correspondent shoes he looked elegant

Speaking in Arabic in hushed tones so as not to disturb the prayers Gazelle opened the meeting. The younger men didn't have names - they were simply called by letters of the alphabet. The main thing this small group had in common was they were all members of the Muslim Brotherhood and adherents to the cause:

Allah is our objective

The Qur'an is the Constitution

The Prophet is our leader

Jihad is our way

Death for the sake of Allah is our wish.

Part of the reason these men were selected was, despite them being a mix of Shia and Sunni Muslims, they had no sectarian views. This was essential for there must be no religious disputes in the organisation - harmony must prevail. Another important reason for selection was that none of the group was known to the police or security services.

Reverting to impeccable English Gazelle pronounced his mission commanded by the Supreme Commander of the Brotherhood.

"We are instructed to carry out a 'terrorist atrocity', as the infidels would say, of great magnitude in the UK. Before we develop this idea, further recruitment has to take place, which is where this group comes in - the first stage."

He continued. "We require new recruits - they must be white, non-Muslim radicalised converts to Islam. They must speak English with or without an accent, and most importantly they must be believers in the Brotherhood and its objectives. Like you they also need to be non-sectarian. Do any of you have any ideas?"

The group considered this for a moment or two before the second member, B, spoke.

"I have a few colleagues that may fit the picture, like me they all work in the banking sector and are more interested in making money than religious in-fighting."

Another, the fifth member - E spoke next to say he had some suitable contacts in Scotland. Various ideas came forward from others. Gazelle was pleased.

"Before you disperse and contact your colleagues we have to talk about security and communication. We will not be using computers under any circumstances. We will be using mobile telephones that are to be turned on only at specified times - these times will be provided with each telephone. They are to be used for text only using your initial letter when sending – your contact number is already in your telephone that I will give you shortly. For back-up we will use that very old system - the Dead Letter Drop. Therefore, I require each of you to set up a third-party mailbox to be checked regularly being mindful that you are not being watched. Do any of you have problems with this?"

"What do we do if we're successful in locating recruits?" asked A.

"Today is Tuesday. I shall be here each day next week and will interview the candidates, each interview will last about forty minutes. Of course you mustn't tell them the details that you know of this project - they will have to take you on good faith. When you introduce them they must have a false name.

"Each candidate must be accompanied by only one of you - there should be no more of you here at the time of the interview. You must liaise with each other as to day and time and inform me. I do not want the group coming here together here at any one time to avoid suspicion by anyone observing the comings and goings at this Mosque.

"Finally, for the time being, is the question of funding. This should not be an issue provided any financial requirement is authorised by me alone. All expenses will be reimbursed. "

There were no more questions. Gazelle handed out mobile telephones each with a note regarding the time it was to be turned on. Prayers had just finished and as the congregation broke up the meeting dispersed, he wished them good luck in their mission. He stayed behind for twenty minutes or so before heading off for his home not far away.

Appointments were made for the following week. There were four potential candidates, all white, British radicalised Islamic converts.

The interviews took place with good humour and grace. It came down to two out of the four being selected - by chance an Englishman and a Scotsman. The former put up by A, the latter by C. The usual security and background checks had to be carried out - this took the rest of the week. There was no shortage of adherents to the cause willing to help with any requests by the Brotherhood. They had people working for the police, local authorities, HMRC and even within government - like a spy network.

Stage one was now completed.

The Muslim Brotherhood is a mysterious organisation. Some believe it is the political wing of ISIL but, like its leadership, no one really knows. Something similar could be said of Gazelle.

There are rumours that he isn't Muslim at all but a Christian descended from Prester John and very senior in the Brotherhood – he seems to be feared. Certainly his appearance is strange and perhaps he originated in Abyssinia and not Aleppo. The only thing that could be confirmed was that he was a fine consultant surgeon.

Chapter

3

Another meeting was fixed by mobile text message for the following Friday - always a good day because the prayers attracted a large crowd of worshippers, they acted as excellent cover for those attending the meeting.

A different venue was to be used - another Mosque, but this time in central London. The location was given in the text as simply the area the meeting was to be held - such as Kensington. All had been briefed that until further notice the meeting would always be in the Mosque of the chosen area on a Friday, just before 11 o'clock.

This particular Mosque had a good size meeting room to one side. After the normal greetings by the Imam the group, including the two new recruits, was shown to the room.

The meeting began with greetings to all and a briefing for the new recruits. Gazelle got them up to speed and explained the processes the others had been given - these two were to be known for the time being as G and H.

"At this stage I would like all of you except A, C, G and H to leave, you will be contacted again to help with stage three. Thank you for your assistance so far," and raising his hand in benediction - "May Allah be with you."

With that, after the normal courtesies, the excluded members of the group left. The prayers were ongoing as they walked out of the meeting room, two of them stayed to pray.

Those remaining sat at the boardroom type table with Gazelle at the head.

"I can tell you that we are but one of three groups studying targets to attack. The other two groups are looking at infrastructure and politicians. Our task is to find a suitable target in the Royal family

There was an absolutely stunned silence in the room - the jaws of three of the group had dropped. The shock didn't manifest itself because of an abhorrence of the idea of killing a Royal, but the sheer audacity of considering it.

Gazelle cleared his throat and sipped from a glass of water before continuing.

"Before discussing a specific individual I wish to talk about our research into the project. Currently we believe that trying to execute a target in or around any of the London Palaces - Buckingham, St James, Clarence House, Kensington Palace and others including Windsor will present great difficulties. The security level at each is extremely high and we calculate there would only be a 20% chance of success at best. We have had surveillance at each of the Palaces for the past three months and this confirms our thoughts. Additionally, our friends in the IRA have provided us with their own research - whilst a lot of it is out of date there is some useful information in the file which you will receive a copy of.

"We have concluded that our best chances of success lie in the countryside - namely Sandringham in Norfolk, or Balmoral in Scotland. I wish you to split into two teams to research these locations and provide information on them. G and H will select which area they want to cover - A and C will be their link-men with all communications going through them. I suggest all written messages are sent by dead letter drop confirmed by a text to alert the recipient.

"Now, false identities for G and H will be prepared. G, what is your given name?"

"Seamus."

"Okay, your new name will be Seamus Gallagher."

"H, and your given name?"

"Wolfe."

"Is that WOLF?"

"It has an E on the end, as in General Wolfe: he beat the French in Canada. I've had to live with my father's eccentricity, he was obsessed with the General and his exploits."

"Okay, you will become Wolfe Hammond. In a day or two I will provide you with all the requisite paperwork - passports, licences, utility bills, several debit cards, etcetera. Included will be your new addresses and keys for the duration of this exercise, obviously you do not have to reside there all the time, they will be back-up for your new identities. You will be notified when the papers are ready.

"If you ever receive a text message 'LEAVE' then you must vacate your vehicle or your new address immediately, I do mean immediately as you will be in danger

"One more thing before I ask you to select who is going where - here are the keys to two Land Rover Discovery vehicles, these are provided because they will fit in with the rural environment you will be working in - they will not stand out as unusual. This is where you collect them from but not at the same time. All relevant paperwork, insurance etcetera will be in the vehicles that will be registered in your names at your new addresses." He handed over the keys and a slip of paper with the name and address of the garage they had to go to, it was in Finsbury Park.

Hammond and Gallagher had a brief conversation before Hammond spoke up. Ironically the Scotsman decided on Norfolk and Hammond selected Scotland. The former had been married to a woman from Fakenham in Norfolk and had spent a lot of time in the area. The latter, after years of salmon fishing and stalking, knew Scotland well. The matter was decided.

"Hammond, you will know this but for the benefit of the others both these venues are famous sporting Estates therefore they have certain advantages. 'Let' days are available on both Estates and participants are vetted - this gives the Royals income. Norfolk is renowned for its English Partridge and Scotland for its Red deer, Salmon and Grouse. It is not unusual for strangers to be around at either location - this causes difficulties with their security.

"All family members are accompanied by Police of the Royal Protection Command – S014, they are always armed. Any vehicles carrying members of the family are armoured.

"Around August through to October the Royal family use Balmoral and later in November, through to and including Christmas, they use Sandringham. Are there any questions?"

"Yes," said Gallagher. "How do you propose to carry out an execution?"

"The method - that will be decided after your research is completed and will form the basis of a future meeting."

A spoke next. "What if the target cannot be executed alone - in other words if other members of the family get involved does that restrict us?"

"No, if it's possible it would be a better outcome, but we will discuss that further at the next meeting too."

"Gallagher there is one more thing you should know about Norfolk. The Duke of Cambridge, Prince William, and his family have recently moved into their country home - it's called Anmer Hall on the Sandringham Estate, but we know absolutely nothing about it."

Handing Gallagher and Hammond their copies of the IRA report Gazelle spoke again.

"Well, that is your brief. If you have no further questions then you should be on your way. It is important that once you arrive at your destination that you text, at the appropriate time if possible - there will be difficulties with reception in both areas. The message to be sent to your link should be 'INSIT' with your initial at the end.

With no further questions the meeting broke up and the participants left, Gazelle gave his customary benediction. The prayer session had finished and the group walked out individually at two minute intervals.

Forty-eight hours later Hammond and Gallagher were on their way to their destinations. They had collected their vehicles and papers and Hammond checked his new address out; Gallagher didn't. They returned to their respective homes to pack belongings and put their arrangements in place - both thought their mission would take three or four days.

14

The purpose of the mission, and the fact they were going to be using the same modus operandi and asking similar questions, was that they would familiarise themselves with the locations with a view to finding a suitable spot to carry out an execution, and to suggest a method.

Chapter

3

Hammond, real name Dean, lived in Essex. The single, self-employed photographer had no difficulties in being away. He packed his camera equipment partly as cover and also to take advantage of any shots that became available in the stunning scenery of the destination that he knew of. As usual, when he was going to Scotland, he also packed his outdoor gear and his thumb-stick.

The slim 29 year old introvert was just under 6 feet tall, brown hair and grey eyes, very ordinary looking really but, he had the most engaging smile - a winner with women probably. But, he was moody, had that disgusting habit of chewing his nails and suffered bouts of depression.

He was an only child; born in Germany, both his parents were from a military background. Much to his father's disappointment Hammond didn't show the slightest interest in following in his footsteps, instead he chose a more passive pursuit - religion.

On one of his father's tours of duty with the King's Own Scottish Borderers he was posted to Colchester and the family decided to stay there. Hammond did well at school and went on to Durham University to read Theology. All went well until he discovered girls - at around the same time he received an inheritance from an aunt and that's where his education came off the rails. He took to drugs and all night parties, left university prematurely and bought a flat in Clerkenwell in London - he got in with a Bohemian crowd and spent a couple of years photographing and bedding beautiful women before selling his flat and returning to Colchester.

An unlikely convert to Islam, Hammond just didn't fit and he'd never expressed any interest to his friends, until he read T E Lawrence and saw the film Lawrence of Arabia - this sparked his initial fascination with the subject.

He started to read the Qur'an and became immersed in its contents. In effect he seemed to be brainwashing himself. From an early age he'd developed a strong sense of justice and he like the way Islam handled this issue in particular - literally an eye for an eye under Sharia law. He had empathy for the cause to get rid of the infernal westerners who had raped their Arab lands for centuries - the Ottomans, the British and French and latterly the Americans. Early on he didn't visit Mosques or converse with scholars on the subject, he simply read and explored the religion alone - he kept himself to himself.

One day by chance he was commissioned to take photographs at a wedding, a friend had recommended him. As it turned out the client was a Muslim doctor living in London. They became friends and the doctor instigated Hammond's next stage of the journey to Islam. He introduced him to various scholars and visited many Mosques. Eventually he came into contact with the Muslim Brotherhood - the doctor was a member. One thing led to another and a year or two later he was inducted into the Islamic faith and joined the Brotherhood.

He became an avid convert. Radicalised early on he attended Madrasas in Bosnia and Pakistan and jihadist training camps in Syria and Iraq, undergoing weapons training at the latter. On the outside he seemed a calm individual, almost shy but, inside his head he was in turmoil - he bit his nails to the quick.

He took his normal route to Scotland. It's all pretty dull until you get beyond Perth and then Blairgowrie. The vast landscape begins to change – you arrive in the Cairngorms National Park - snow on the peaks. Here, if you are lucky, you might see a Golden Eagle, Mountain Hares, Ptarmigan, Peregrine Falcons and, of course, Red Deer. Dropping down from the pass he arrived at Braemar where they have the Highland Games gathering attended by the Royal Family each year

- he needed to have a look at the site. After finding somewhere to stay that would be his first job in the morning.

Most of the hotels in Braemar were closed, the few that were open didn't appeal so he drove on in the direction of Balmoral. He had stayed in a charming little hotel by the side of the River Dee on the route a few years ago, that too was closed. He continued to Ballater where he found a number of choice establishments, all open - presumably for the Spring fishermen - he booked into what he thought looked the best.

It was 8 hours since he had left Essex. He had a walk around the charming town to get his circulation working properly. There was a chill in the air and it was getting dark as he returned to his hotel to settle in the bar that had a glowing log fire, very welcoming he thought. He ordered a pint of beer and a whisky chaser - it was now just after 6pm. Muslims are forbidden to drink alcohol but many, particularly converts to Islam, ignore the prohibition - Hammond liked his whisky, beer and wine.

He checked quickly, his mobile telephone had a good signal, scheduled to turn it on at 6.45 he would watch the drinking beforehand. The bar began filling up with locals and ruddy, weather-beaten faced fisherman chilled to the bone no doubt after a day on the river in the Spring. As copious amounts of beer and whisky were being dispensed, talk of the day's sport began in a very animated way with everyone contributing it seemed. At this point he went to his room turned his phone on and sent the text - 'INSITH'. There were no messages. He wasn't gone long before he returned to the bar, his stool was still vacant.

Hammond had formed his main cover plan during the journey north. He was in that part of Scotland to research a gift to his (dead) father for his 60th. A keen shot and fisherman his long held ambition was to complete a McNab - Hammond's destination was the place to do it. The aim is to shoot a Red deer, a Grouse and catch a Salmon in a twenty-four hour period.

John McNab was a character from the John Buchan 1925 novel of the same name. On a good sporting adventure in the Highlands McNab achieves it and the idea caught on in real life - to this day prizes for the achievement are still given - some of them valuable.

Various people chatted to him at the bar - mainly they belonged to a large party up for a week chasing Springers - large early salmon - no luck so far they reported. They were all friendly enough, but he enjoyed his own fishing parties enormously rather than those of others.

At 7.45 dinner was announced. The hotel was very busy and there were going to be two sittings in the restaurant, his was the second, an hour later.

The bar began to empty and soon there were only four people left, he sat alone. He'd established that the man he took for the barman was in fact the owner.

Wolfe Hammond introduced himself to Archie the owner and they started chatting.

He gave the outline of the reason for his visit.

"Do you know how I could get in and have a look at the Games Gathering showground? I would love to see and get a feel for it as it will be an important event in the birthday celebrations if I can pull all this together."

"You need to see Jimmy James who looks after it, he's an old friend of mine - I'll call him and ask for you."

"Thank you. Another question if I may. Who is the factor on the Balmoral Estate and how do I contact him?"

"That'll be Colonel Fergusson, but you won't get a hold of him until the morning, I'll give you his number." He scribbled it down and slid it across the bar to Hammond.

They carried on chatting and Hammond had another Scotch before it was time to go through and dine. He had an excellent meal - Gravlax followed with Pigeon breasts. By the time he'd finished it was just gone 10 o'clock - he was tired after a long day and decided to go to bed rather than get back with the crowd that had returned to the bar. At the foot of the stairs to his room he bumped into Archie.

"I've spoken to Jimmy James and he's prepared to take you to the showground in the morning. He'll be waiting at 9 30 in a red Subaru on the forecourt of the first hotel on the left as you go into Braemar."

"That's really kind of you to have done that. Now, after an excellent meal I'm off to my bed, many thanks and goodnight."

Climbing the stairs he decided he would read the IRA report into their findings at Balmoral. Entering his room and just about to take out the report hidden in the lining of his hold-all he changed his mind. He wasn't going to read it until he'd completed his own research - he didn't want to be influenced by someone else's work. Instead he wrote up his truncated notes of the days events, something he would do each day. He closed the diary and returned it to his bag removing a small prayer rug as he did so. After washing and prayers he went to bed.

Chapter

4

Hammond sat in his Land Rover with the heater going full blast to defrost the vehicle. He watched the fishing party leave in their vehicles, their long salmon rods bouncing on the roof and bonnet mounted clamps as if in excited anticipation of the days sport. It was a beautiful morning but there had been a hard overnight frost and it looked as if the roads would be icy.

He'd breakfasted well and was going off to meet Jimmy James in Braemar. Before he left his hotel he called Colonel Fergusson to make an appointment for 2 pm at Balmoral.

The red Subaru was outside the hotel as promised, a short wizened old man in a kilt stood by it. Hammond got out of his vehicle and walked over to him proffering his hand - James had a withered right arm and shook with his left hand.

Jimmy was not the most communicative person Hammond had ever met, he was nice enough but monosyllabic. They spent about an hour going around the showground site and any one of Hammond's questions was dealt with in one of three ways - yes, no or don't know. The place didn't seem the least suitable as a killing ground - too exposed, but he took some photographs anyway and made a mental note to get hold of some videos of the Highland Games.

He dropped James off at his vehicle, thanked him and continued back to his hotel and beyond, he wanted to have a look at Crathie Church on the Royal Estate. He wasn't hopeful that would be suitable either but he needed to assure himself, again he would get hold of some film footage.

There were no signs of spring this far north, the hills were still covered in snow and the skiing industry was having a good season. The Church was locked but he walked around the graveyard and concluded his thoughts were correct - the place wasn't suited at all to what he had in mind.

By the time he'd returned to his car the sun had gone and the sky was now leaden grey, it was 11.15. He was going to reconnoiter the few roads in the area starting with the route to Tomintoul, the temperature gauge on the dashboard read minus 3 - it was looking like snow.

He made his way to the A939, a route he used often when going to fish the River Deveron in the summer but, he'd never used it at this time of year before. Normally the single track road through a desolate moor was deserted, but today it was incredibly busy with skiers on their way to the Lecht ski centre midway on the route.

On a clear day you could see perhaps ten miles ahead, ideal sniper territory if only you knew when the victim was going to be using it, but of course you never would which ruled that idea out; nonetheless he stopped in several places and took photographs.

He'd overheard a conversation in the bar last night. Apparently members of the Royal family would go, unaccompanied, shopping for gifts in Tomintoul where there were one or two specialist shops. But, knowing who was going and when was in the lap of the Gods.

After a brief look around the village he bought a sandwich and can of drink from the bakers then retraced his journey toward Balmoral for his 2pm appointment. The road was very quiet now, the skiers had gone home or they were lying low waiting for the imminent snowstorm to pass - the only vehicle he saw during the twenty-five mile journey was a snow plough/gritter.

The storm started just as he approached the driveway to Balmoral Estate office - snowflakes the size of coffee saucers, visibility almost zero. He negotiated the drive at a snail's pace and pulled up outside the Scottish Baronial building, a miniature of the 'big house' - it was only a few yards to the entrance but he was covered in snow when he went through the large semi-glazed door to reception. He shook himself off, brushed his clothing down in the vestibule and then went into the warm reception. The tiled floor, cedar panelling and counter area and log fire gave the room an inviting aura - he was early.

Janet, the friendly receptionist asked Hammond to be seated in one of the armchairs by the fire - the Colonel wasn't back from lunch but should be shortly. Arriving a couple of minutes later he trailed a flurry of snow like a wraith. Extending his hand he said, "You must be Mr Hammond, I'm Fergusson," and they shook hands. "Please come in," as he opened his office door. On the way in he asked Janet for coffee.

This large room doubled as the Estate archive library and an office. It was a bigger version of the reception, and was lined with floor to ceiling bookshelves; it had a scholarly feel to it and of course a log fire blazing away. The coffee came in and they settled themselves in comfortable armchairs next to the fire.

"Fine weather you've brought with you Mr Hammond!" They both chuckled. "Now, how can I help?"

Hammond had been studying the factor while he dealt with coffee. In his late fifties, tall, slim and distinguished looking - every inch a military man not unlike his late father in appearance. He was a friendly and had warmth that was unusual, in Hammond's experience, of military types - he looked very capable.

Before answering the question Hammond glanced at one of the windows, it was as if it had been painted with whitewash, there must be a blizzard blowing he thought.

"How long do you think this storm will last Colonel?"

"Och, not long, it'll soon blow itself out."

"Good. I had visions of being snowed in for days."

He related his quest for his father's birthday present that should include the opportunity of a McNab and a visit to the Highland Games.

"When are you thinking of Mr Hammond?"

"September next year."

"That should be fine. Let me explain how it works here. I would suggest you make it a long weekend, Friday to Monday inclusive. The Friday morning to be spent with your father having some practice under the eyes of our head ghillie, he's a stickler for safety. If for any reason your father fails on that front the booking is cancelled and a refund less 10% is made.

"Assuming there are no problems then it's a visit to the games on the Saturday. Monday will start bright and early when he can try for a stag followed by a Grouse or two. The remains of the twenty-four hours can be devoted to catching a salmon. We had three successful McNabs' here last year. If this works for you then I will write to you with details and costings - please leave your address with Janet when you leave."

"That sounds perfect Colonel. Just one question - is it possible for me to see the ground my father will be shooting over and the beat on the river that he'll be fishing while I'm here?"

"Normally I would say no but, as it happens, I'm going to check the Grouse butts tomorrow and you'd be welcome to join me. It'll mean an early start - here at 0700 hours - warm clothing, a flask and packed lunch are essential."

"I'd love to, it sounds very interesting."

As he finished speaking the sun came out, it's powerful rays directly in his eyes through one of the windows - like a laser, it hurt.

Hammond left, he stumbled with eyes screwed up through four or five inches of snow that had fallen, the sun was blinding, he was desperate for his sunglasses that he'd left in the car. After clearing the windows he got into the vehicle and looked round - the landscape looked stunningly beautiful under the now clear blue sky. It took a while to get back to the hotel - there had been three accidents and snow ploughs delayed progress, by the time he got there he was starving.

When he left the hotel next morning dawn was approaching, the temperature had risen according to the dashboard thermometer - it was plus 5 degrees - positively balmy Hammond thought. Except where it had drifted the snow had mostly gone on the low ground but in the half-light it was visible on the hills. He arrived at the Estate office early but the Colonel was waiting for him in his Land Rover Defender that Hammond, with his kit, got into.

They set off into the hills climbing steadily, at the tree line they got to the snow, here it lay about 6 inches deep and the sturdy Land Rover came into its own. They eventually arrived at a barn, open on one side, containing half a dozen Argocats and two Hanomags all immaculate in dark green livery and all lined up waiting to go - they were about 1500 feet above sea level and in every direction the snow lay crisp and even.

After transferring to one of the Argocats they continued climbing, they couldn't see the track because of the snow but were guided by snow poles alongside. The Argocat is nothing more than a plastic bathtub on eight independently sprung and driven wheels - noisy and very uncomfortable, with no weather equipment you are exposed to the elements. However, its ability to negotiate this type of terrain in these conditions was unmatched.

Conversation was impossible while they were on the move because of the noise but they were each weighing the other up. Fergusson was thinking his companion was okay and suitable to be a short-term tenant on the Estate, but his habit of chewing his nails irritated him. Hammond was delighted to have the opportunity to see the lie of the land. Wading through the snow almost above the tops of their Wellingtons was difficult but the butts had to be inspected. They were just about half way through the task when they stopped for their lunch - the sun was shining and there was a hint of warmth from it - it was noon.

They pulled up by a bothy and went it, the fire was set, all it needed was to be lit which Fergusson did - it was soon ablaze and they sat by it eating their lunches.

"Security must be a nightmare for you when the family is in residence," Hammond asked rhetorically.

"No, we're used to it - years of practice and having 100 pairs of eyes helps."

"But having armed strangers around the place must present risks surely?"

"Everyone is vetted as you are being right now. In addition we have, in season, 100 staff and the place crawls with armed coppers when the family is here - the chances of penetrating the security cordon are zero."

Hammond didn't want to arouse suspicions by persisting with his questions. He'd got the answers he needed, those, with his observations so far were giving him little hope this was a suitable location for an assassination. Maybe the fishing will offer an opportunity he was thinking.

They finished their lunch and continued with the inspection, Fergusson seemed satisfied with the recent repairs that had been carried out - he had demanding clients and if there were complaints he would soon hear about it. By the time they'd finished if was 4pm, the temperature was plummeting as the sky clouded over - Fergusson predicted more snow.

As they pulled into the barn to change vehicles Hammond was numb with cold and it had started to snow lightly. Fergusson's Land Rover soon warmed up as they drove down from the moor to the Estate office, it was just getting dark when they arrived. Too late in the day to have a look at the river he asked Fergusson if he could do it tomorrow, he agreed and they went into the office for a permit.

Hammond drove back to his hotel in steady snowfall but, it wasn't settling. The hotel was surprisingly quiet - the two fishing parties staying there had been invited to dinner by their fishing beat owners. After bathing and prayers he took the IRA report from his bag and went down to the dining room. He ordered a gin and tonic and his meal and settled down to read the report. It wasn't a very thick document and its conclusions were very much in line with his own - no clear opportunities.

He chuckled to himself when he got to the section titled 'Recommendations'. A bomb, planted in the tourist season and on a very long fuse was thought to be too indiscriminate - since when were the IRA fussed about such things? Snipers were considered but the same problem kept cropping up - where was the target going to be and when?

Over breakfast he decided he would check out of the hotel and once he'd had a look at the river drive south. He'd bought a postcard and first class stamp at reception and scribbled a note asking for CDs of the Games and Balmoral to be located and delivered to his London address - he addressed the postcard it to his link's dead letter drop.

Hammond drove to the river on a miserable grey morning, at least it was mild. He found the ghillie with a client fisherman outside a hut on a bend in the river. When asked he produced his permit - the ghillie wasn't over-helpful so he wandered down the river looking with envy at some of the superb pools, he'd never fished the Dee.

Some of the river banks were steeply wooded and offered good cover for a sniper but the same old question came up - when would the target be there - impossible to know without the crucial intelligence. The question nagged at him all the way back to Colchester.

Chapter

5

Gallagher was an enigma. No one knew who he was or where he'd come from – he was known as just Seamus. The Gallagher surname was given him by Gazelle. He was vouched for by his link man, E the banker, who confirmed he was a member of the Muslim Brotherhood. It was rumoured that Seamus was the mastermind behind the failed bomb attack on Glasgow airport in 2007.

He was around fifty years old and very ordinary really. With fair hair with a reddish tinge, grey eyes and about five feet ten inches tall he looked very strong and fit, as if he worked out regularly. He spoke with a slight brogue, difficult to say whether Scottish or Irish.

Leaving Glasgow and after a similar length of journey to Hammonds' he arrived in Norfolk.

He'd booked a room in a small hotel in the village of Flitcham, about three miles from Sandringham. As he came into the village, tired as he was after the long journey, he managed to avoid flattening two cock pheasants that ran in front of his car squabbling. Their gaudy bronze and gold plumage made him think of a couple of old Queens, the sort you used to see promenading in Hope Street, Glasgow or Soho, London.

His cover story, thought through on the journey down, was that he'd been to the funeral of an uncle in Fakenham and thought he'd take a couple of days off from his carpentry business and see the Sandringham area. He was thinking of taking a let days shooting on the Estate with some of his mates and he needed advice. He'd read of the famous English Partridge days in the past on the Estate laid out for the purpose by King Edward V11. He had the outline of the idea before he left and managed to read parts of the history of the great Estate before

29

leaving, it just gave him the gist - he didn't want to appear to have any knowledge.

After checking into the hotel he walked the perimeter of the building to see if he could get a signal for his mobile - he was due to send his message at 6 o'clock, slightly earlier than Hammond - he couldn't get even get one bar so he gave up. He went inside to the hotel bar, ordered a pint and sat on a stool next to the only other customer whose old yellow Labrador lay at his feet.

By good fortune his neighbour, he discovered while chatting to him, was the head-keeper of the Sandringham estate. He'd introduced himself as Sean Gallagher and gave the outline of his reason to be in the area. Jack Christmas, as the keeper was called, and he hit it off immediately. He wangled an invitation to accompany the keeper on his rounds of the beats to have a look around the day after tomorrow, they were to meet at 9 o'clock by the estate office - he was given directions.

The following day, armed with his OS map, he decided to have a look around the area starting with Prince William's property at Anmer. Heading north and climbing out of the village he turned left onto an unmarked lane at the summit just as he got a signal on his mobile, he pulled onto the verge and sent his INSTG text.

Looking up and before moving off he could see a hive of activity with a black, unmarked police Discovery parked ahead of him, its occupants were watching him. This narrow lane ran down the west side of the Anmer estate and workmen were installing a screen of woven willow panels each about six feet square to shield the view of the Hall from the lane, in addition they were laying a blackthorn and hawthorn hedge – an excellent barrier when fully grown.

He checked on his map and the belt of woodland ahead of him was not shown, the map must be 50 or 60 years out of date he thought. Gauging the distance from the main road to the woodland at around

800 metres he moved off slowly trying to avoid the workmen, as he passed the police vehicle they followed him, almost certainly checking his vehicle details on the police radio.

A tractor was blocking the lane ahead and he had to stop at a section that hadn't yet been screened. He was able to get a good look at the Hall sitting in a natural depression - the handsome red brick Georgian house was beautifully located with the Church to its left. The block of woodland was about 300 metres deep and the distance from its edge to the mansion was a further 800/1000 metres. The tractor moved off and he continued with the police vehicle behind him – they didn't make any attempt to stop him.

At the T junction he turned right and the police left. Now on the north side of the Hall he continued to the main road and just as he cleared the village of Anmer he came across about a dozen vehicles parked up. The occupants were standing in a group looking south with a variety of binoculars and some with cameras – he wondered what they were looking at and, out of curiosity, stopped and asked them – Twitchers. They were looking for an American white crowned Sparrow, a rare visitor to UK shores. This gave Gallagher food for thought.

At the crossroads he turned right again heading along the east side of the Estate back to where he'd started from. It had turned into a fine day after a damp and misty morning and he was heading for Sandringham. The house was closed to the public but he looked around the park before heading the short distance to the coast – he had an idea beginning to form in his head.

After making notes on his map of the estimated distances between the main road and the Hall he dined in the hotel, it wasn't very busy but the food was excellent. Complete and utter rubbish he said to himself as he closed the IRA file, a bunch of amateurs. Apparently there was an attempt on Prince Charles' life on a shoot at Sandringham some years ago, it was abandoned, but no reason was given.

Gazelle, with a glass of malt whiskey in hand and smoking a cigar was pacing on the fine Tabriz rug in front of his hearth, was slightly concerned that he hadn't had a signal from Norfolk - it was 11 o'clock in the evening. He was flying to Cairo tomorrow and wanted to be confident that this stage of his plan was underway when he reported to his superiors. His main worry was that instead of the project being in the heads and hands of a very few close colleagues there was now a much larger group that knew.

At just after 10.30 in the morning, while driving to the airport, his mobile rang - INSTG.

After a great Norfolk breakfast Gallagher set off to meet Jack Christmas, it was a beautiful morning.

Take the road to Sandringham, go past the Royal stud and turn left at the T junction, then take the second entrance on the right he'd been told by Christmas. He pulled up outside a large Victorian house, the Estate office and the keeper was waiting on the door steps.

They set of in the keeper's Defender and headed towards the Wash at Wolferton, he stopped by a mule (a small all-terrain vehicle) to speak to one of his under-keepers, standing beside one of the blue grain feeders.

Jack was a garrulous character with a strong Norfolk dialect, sometimes difficult to understand. He wasn't very tall and reminded Gallagher of a Jack Russell Terrier but he chuckled a lot.

"How long have you worked here Jack?"

"Oh, most of my life I should think, I got this from the Queen for fifty years service," proudly showing the heavy gold Rolex on his wrist, bling didn't suit him. "This area is where we do the wildfowling," pointing he said, "you can see the hides over there,"

Gallagher was asking varied questions most of which were out of ignorance, all he really wanted to do was get the lie of the land. This was a lovely landscape on a fine day looking across the Wash to Lincolnshire but it must be bleak and miserable in the winter he was thinking

"The Estate is just over 20,000 acres but a lot of that is woodland. It's a wild bird shoot, in other words we don't raise any game; all birds are born and roam free which makes them harder to shoot."

Apart from Christmas there are eight under-keepers who, when there isn't a shoot going on, are employed to feed the birds at the many blue feeding stations and control vermin.

"It must be very expensive to shoot here what will all the staff."

"Aye, it is. It's around £40 per bird. Whoever takes the shooting for a let day contracts for X number of birds. If they miss them that's their fault not ours, I count the number of shots and they're allowed four shots per bird. Because they are wild birds most are missed."

"Does the family shoot a lot?"

"Quite a bit, especially around the Christmas period."

And so they carried on driving all over the estate. It was lovely country with enormous amounts of wild life that all looked in excellent condition. It was a long day and Gallagher, after a few pints with the keeper and an early meal, went to bed, he had a long drive tomorrow.

Chapter

6

On this occasion the meeting was being held in a windowless air conditioned room in the bowels of MI5 headquarters in Thames House. There were four people present in the room: Max Simmonds, head of MI5, Ned Boswell, head of the Police Protection Command SO14, Betine McLeod, head of SIS and Maria Webley, Max Simmonds' secretary. The meetings were held on a regular basis and the venue changed each time. Apart from the red emergency button on the grey wall the room was featureless; there were twelve clear plastic chairs and a Perspex top rectangular table but no adornments. Understandably, given the circumstances, the three heads all looked tired and under pressure.

Simmonds and Boswell had served in Afghanistan together, the former in Military Intelligence the latter as a Colonel in the Special Forces. McLeod had been in the diplomatic corps, she had been at university with Simmonds and they graduated at the same time – all in their fifties they knew each other well.

As a matter of course, in a well established procedure, activity reports for the week are recovered from all Royal Estates and palaces, this is organised by Ned Boswell. After he has analysed the reports they are discussed in these meetings. The reports are accompanied with CCTV footage, where available, along with comments and observations from Estate and palace staff – it's a bit old-fashioned but the system works. All information is logged on Boswell's database. Early Spring is a quiet time for tourism and the reports are generally thin. This week nothing stood out and all checks on the individuals identified were negative.

McLeod was sitting back in her chair staring at the ceiling. "Are you still with us Betine?" asked Ned Boswell in a jocular way.

"Oh, I am sorry, I was miles away." She was fixed on the grainy black and white CCTV image of a man in front of her - it was taken in the reception area of a small hotel in Norfolk. "I'm sure I've met this guy somewhere but, I'm damned if I can remember where. Does anyone else recognise him?" They said no.

There was, attached to the image, the guy's name – Seamus Gallagher and the registration of his vehicle, both in the hotel's register. He'd paid the £330 bill in cash. He and his vehicle, a Land Rover Discovery, had been checked out without result, by two Protection Command officers when it was seen near the Duke of Cambridge's residence, all seemed legitimate.

Did the image lingering in McLeod's head mean the man was a villain? No, of course not, he could be a man that worked in the garage where they serviced her car or even the dustman, she tried to dismiss the image without success but it troubled her. Her nagging headache probably didn't help.

Simmonds got home just after 10pm, a staff driver had dropped him at a Chinese near to where he lived, he was a regular there and even though it was very busy they found him a table. He got home, poured himself a Scotch, sat down and promptly fell asleep.

His wife and son were on holiday at their cottage in Cornwall - he should have been with them but was simply snowed under at work and socially. The crick in his neck woke him, he felt dreadful and very cold. It was still dark, 4.30am. It was too late to go to bed and too early to go to work. A long hot bath and a cup of coffee made him feel a lot better. By the time he'd had some breakfast the sun was coming up but there had been a sharp frost, T S Elliot was right, April is the cruellest month of all. As he left the house a blast of cold air hit him but a brisk walk to the tube quickly warmed him up. By the time he got to Thames House just before 7am the frost had gone. He walked into his office, as he did the secure line on his desk rang – it was Commander James Tyson at Scotland Yard.

"Good morning Max, I'm glad you're in early - how are you?"

"Well thanks James – I hope you are too. What have you got for me?"

Many of Simmonds' leads came through Tyson.

"We had a tip off about illegal immigrants and raided a garage in Finsbury Park a couple of hours ago. We arrested six people and among them was one Alim Badru who is flagged by MI5 on the PNC system."

"Did you remove anything from the premises?"

"We're still searching, I'll let you have a manifest when we've finished. I'll call you when we've done."

"Thanks James, I'll send someone over to sit-in on your interview with this guy if you don't mind."

"Be my guest."

Simmonds pulled up the file for Badru – he was classified as low risk. He'd been interviewed after being involved in a student protest several years ago but not charged, he'd fallen below the radar since.

Natalie Stone, or Nat as she preferred to called, was a new intern - she'd been with MI5 for six months and, under Simmonds' wing, was progressing well. Simmons tasked her with liaising with Commander Tyson instructing her to take notes but stay silent.

Tall for a woman and with jet black hair, bob cut, the thirty year old was pretty and elegant. She had a slightly Oriental appearance from her mother who, like her, was born in Hong Kong. Her father was Scottish, a civil engineer. Both parents were killed in a car crash on their way to see her when she was at university in Newcastle, she had no siblings – it was a devastating period for her.

She did well at university graduating with a degree in psychology and then joined the police. Home was a bijou one bedroom flat on the High Street in Walthamstow overlooking the market – she loved the hustle and bustle of the market when it was open, otherwise it was surprisingly quiet.

Nat had a passion – motorbikes, big powerful ones. She'd learned to ride her father's BSA Bantam when she was 10 years old living, at that time, in Borneo. She held a motor vehicle and motorcycle licence but had never bothered with a car apart from a short period after university.

She split up with her boyfriend about 18 months previously and took it badly. To compensate, she decided to raid her parent's legacy for the first time and buy a motorbike. Having decided on a classic it took her three months to track down her dream – a Norton Commando 750cc. One owner, and hardly used, it had been garaged for 10 years after the owner died. Advised by a traffic policeman friend who knew about bikes she bought it direct from the widow – it cost £12,500.

Wearing her emerald green leathers with a white crash helmet she looked stunning on the big black bike – she felt sexy. She had a marvellous sense of balance and her slender frame belied her wiriness and physical strength as she deftly handled the bike. One of the market traders in the High Street, a Bangladeshi, had befriended her. He had a secure lock up a few doors along from her flat and allowed her to park her bike there for £20 a week – a bargain. She had access between 0600 and 2000 hours which suited her perfectly. Normally she would go to work on the Tube or by bus – she was what you might call a fair-weather biker.

Just as Simmonds was about to leave the office a call came in, it was Commander Tyson.

"Hello Max. I thought I'd let you know that we've finished with the group we rounded up this morning. I'm sure your girl......Nat I think it was, will give you a debriefing. We searched the garage and flat from top to bottom and found nothing at all but,   we did find that two vehicles that were recorded as sold by the garage are flagged on your system as well as Ned Boswells, I haven't told him yet – will you or should I? We've had to release the suspects as there wasn't anything to charge them with. Both vehicles are Land Rover Discoveries."

"Thanks for this James; I'll tell Ned and Betine McLeod, she'll want to know."

Simmonds asked his secretary to call Boswell and McLeod and arrange a meeting at 0900 the next day before he left, it was 7pm. He was meeting an old friend for a game of squash - he did try to keep fit but failed miserably as was evidenced by his waistline.

Stone had returned and had spent the afternoon studying the information on those that had been rounded up that morning. She had also been trawling the social media looking for the two Land Rover owners without success although of course the names were probably fictitious. However, the Christian name Wolfe did puzzle her, it's not the sort of name you would dream up she was thinking, so perhaps it was real. There were plenty spelt Wolf but none with an e on the end.

The three heads assembled next morning for their meeting. Having cleared it with the others Simmonds asked Stone to join the meeting; he had a project in mind for her.

Having made the introductions they discussed their findings so far. They had a lead regarding the two Land Rovers but, checks on the registered names were a blank. One vehicle had been seen around Balmoral and the other near Sandringham. If it wasn't for the fact they were both bought from the same dealer it would have been passed off as immaterial.

It was decided that the two addresses used in the registration documents would be put under immediate surveillance and any suspects photographed and followed but not detained, MI5 with the uniform branch would do this. Any telephones would be intercepted and thorough checks on the properties would be carried out i.e. who pays the council tax, what post is delivered and what services are connected and who pays for them.

Stone was to make her way to Balmoral; Boswell would inform the factor there that she was coming. She needed to retrace Wolfe Hammond's footsteps and then do the same with Seamus Gallagher's in Norfolk.

Chapter

7

Traffic on the M25 was unusually light. Gazelle checked the departures board and found that his flight to Cairo scheduled for 4pm, nearly three hours time, was on time. He checked in and decided to have lunch air-side – he had a single medium size suitcase and, apart from a book, no hand baggage.

There was the usual tedious wait while he went through security, he was thinking about what he would have for lunch. He removed the contents of his pockets from the X-Ray scanner conveyer and was about to walk off when he was summoned to one side.

"Would you step over here please sir." There were two airport security staff, one a woman, and an armed policeman.

Gazelle bit his lip; he was seething but said nothing.

"Your passport and boarding card please sir?" said the female guard with her hand outstretched.

Gazelle handed them over and the guard studied them carefully.

"You are Sheikh Abdul Mohammed sir?"

"Yes, I am."

"I see you are travelling to Cairo - what is the purpose of your visit sir?"

"I am visiting my family."

"What is your occupation sir?"

He was having difficulty in controlling his temper, nobody but nobody interrogated him like this. "I am a consultant surgeon." he said through gritted teeth.

"Where do you work sir?"

"London, Cairo and Toronto."

"Where do you live sir?"

"In all three places, I have an apartment in each."

"Thank you sir," said the male guard. "Please step into this room as I wish to search you, it'll only take a minute or two."

Again Gazelle had to restrain himself as the guard led him into what might be called a cubicle and shut the door.

"Please remove your shoes and jacket sir."

While Gazelle was complying the guard put on blue latex gloves. He closely examined the shoes and passed a portable scanner over them, then did the same to Gazelle concentrating on the collar to his shirt, waistband and trouser turn-ups – all clear.

"Thank you very much for your cooperation sir, you are now free to go and enjoy your trip to Cairo," said the guard as he handed the passport and boarding pass back.

Gazelle dressed and walked out without speaking - he was still livid. Over lunch, having calmed down, he concluded that he'd been profiled even though the government denied this took place. He was cross because as far as he knew he had never had any dealings with the authorities – has this encounter jeopardised the project? He would have to tell his colleagues in the Brotherhood.

The Air Egypt flight to Cairo International airport was uneventful and on time for a change. It was a fine warm evening as he took a taxi to the Cleopatra Palace hotel by Tahrir Square, it was owned by a friend. He wanted to surprise his sister on her birthday tomorrow evening.

Greg Taylor, one of three SIS operatives based in Cairo, received a call on his mobile while he was having supper in his flat. It was his contact on reception at the Cleopatra telling him that Sheikh Abdul Mohammed had checked in for one night, he was alone.

Taylor had received instructions from London to keep an eye on the Sheikh and report back having photographed him and anyone he met. He should also discreetly do some digging on exactly who this guy is.

At 8 o'clock next morning Taylor was drinking a coffee and pretending to read a newspaper – he was keeping an eye out for the Sheikh – he'd studied an excellent image sent through from London, it shouldn't be difficult to spot him. The reception lobby was busy.

Instead of wearing a suit, the Sheikh appeared wearing traditional Arab clothing with headdress; he went to the reception where he met a man of a similar age wearing a grey suit and a Fez. They walked out of the hotel together and Taylor followed some way behind, it was 10 o'clock – already it was hot.

Cairo, like all other Arab cities Taylor had been in, reeked with the smell of a whole variety of spices and coffee, it was dusty and dirty but vibrant – exciting. He'd been in Arabia for twelve years now.

He could never quite get used to the way many Arab men walk arm-in-arm, but continued following them to the El Shaik Shaban café by the El Azar Mosque – the pavement café was crowded. The two men were looking for a table outside, Taylor walked past and watched from a street corner while they waited; once they were seated he too went and found a table where he could see them both clearly.

Studying his newspaper with one eye he watched them with the other, he ordered a Turkish coffee when a waiter appeared. He managed to take several surreptitious photographs of the two men with his mini-camera.

Slowly but surely the street performer came toward him. Stopping at various tables, it appeared, to the amusement of those sat there that the performer was enjoyed, some people seemed to be laughing and a number were applauding – he was very popular.

He approached the table next to Taylor where there were two pretty young girls, about 20 years old. He'd caught snatches of their conversation and thought they were Dutch.

The performer, an Arab, was juggling three ping-pong size balls with one hand; the girls, wide-eyed, were clearly amazed and started to clap. At that point their animal instinct must have kicked in as they froze at the same moment the performer dropped the balls. He grabbed one of the girls by her hair, produced a knife and slashed her throat from ear to ear. The other girl had her mouth open to scream, she never had a chance as he did the same to her – it all happened in an instant.

There was a moment of silence. The Arab dropped the knife and walked off calmly - then the screaming started and people stampeded away from the café - tables and chairs flying in all directions.

The Sheikh and his colleague hurried away with Taylor in pursuit at a distance. He noticed the sleeve of his linen jacket was splashed with blood from one of the girls; he removed the jacket and folded it over his arm with the stain hidden. Taylor had witnessed some pretty ghastly things during his time in the middle-east, but this took the cake.

As the two men Taylor was following got to a road junction they went in opposite directions. He followed the Sheikh to a bank that he entered and then lost him. After half an hour waiting for him to emerge he went back to the office.

The Sheikh had simply walked through the building as short-cut to the next street; there were two entrances to the building. He went to the nearby ENT (ear, nose and throat) clinic on Hassan El Maamoun Street where he had to carry out two surgical procedures that day - laryngectomies.

As he was leaving the hospital after, to him, two very satisfactory procedures he stopped off at the florists in the foyer – it was 6.30 pm. He bought Lotus flowers, his sister's favourite – it was her birthday and she had no idea he was in Cairo.

The taxi he'd taken pulled into the courtyard of a beautiful villa in the diplomatic district; it was the Sheikh's old family home where his sister, brother-in-law and three nieces lived, it had been in the family for three generations. He instructed the driver to go to the Cleopatra Palace hotel and collect his suitcase and bring it to the villa where he would be staying the night.

He paid the driver, just as he was getting out his mobile bleeped – a text message – '3' is all it said. This was a code for the venue of the Brotherhood meeting in two days time at 2 pm – Delices' café in Alexandria

.

He rang the door bell and was greeted by the nanny/housemaid that he had known for much of his life. As he was shown into the capacious entrance hall his sister appeared trailed by three pretty young giggling girls, they were delighted to see him and she was over the moon with the Lotus flowers.

Taylor had been busy downloading and enhancing the images he'd taken outside the café. He sent them across to his contact in the Egyptian State Security (SSI) to see what, if any, information they had on the two individuals and was waiting to hear back.

The two girls who were brutally murdered that morning were in fact from Finland. Al-Qaeda had claimed responsibility for the atrocity but no one had been arrested according to the news bulletins. Across North Africa and some other parts of the world the public seem inured to this type of senseless slaughter, but the media revel in it.

Gazelle spent a very pleasant day and a bit with his family then left for Alexandria. He took the train for the two and a half hour journey, the first time he'd used that method of transport in Egypt for years – he was impressed; comfortable seats, air conditioning and fast.

The Muslim Brotherhood took security very seriously, they had to. Unlike Al-Qaeda and ISIL they kept a low-profile, they didn't seek publicity. In recent years a number of members had been killed by Egyptian security forces and the Americans.

Pre-arranged, Gazelle turned off his mobile as soon as he'd received the coded call, others going to the meeting would have done the same. He hadn't been to Alexandria for about 15 years and it didn't appear to have changed at all – Delices certainly hadn't, the same cool marble interior and tall Nubian waiters with their blue Fezzes.

There were two armed guards by the entrance and one at the top of the stairs, he was certain there be others in strategic locations around the buildings. He was frisked before being shown into the assembly room. This was a meeting of the strategy and planning committee and the three commanders doing their research into the infrastructure, politicians and the Royal Family in the UK, in a way it was a progress report. No names were used in the meeting in case the building was bugged.

Each of the commanders went through their presentations. It was agreed that the assassination of a politician wouldn't have the impact required therefore that team should link up with the other two groups.

Considerable investigation had gone into the water supply systems in London and Manchester, so far putting toxins into the systems was looking feasible. Further research into the electricity grid was ongoing.

Gazelle made his report. The target had yet to be selected but the venue was probably either Scotland or Norfolk, further information was awaited.

There was some discussion about joining both the infrastructure and Royal family projects together and carrying out both tasks at the same time for maximum impact. A decision on this was deferred until the next meeting in a month's time.

The meeting broke up and Gazelle headed back to Cairo confident that he hadn't been followed. He'd decided not to mention the going over he had received at the airport when leaving London. Apart from that encounter he was certain the authorities were unaware of him.

The SSI had got back to Taylor, they had nothing he didn't already know about the Sheikh and had no record of the individual in a Fez. He reported this to London adding that he had no idea of the whereabouts of the Sheikh but, he was booked on the 2pm flight to Heathrow tomorrow.

Chapter
8

"A what?"

"A DVLA code."

"That sounds like a medical condition. What is it?"

Stone had just arrived at Aberdeen airport and was hiring, or attempting to hire, a car that had been booked for her by the transport manager at Thames House.

The Europcar receptionist chuckled. "No, I'm pleased to say it's not, but you can't hire a car without the code. This is required to establish if you have any motoring convictions. The paper part of your licence is obsolete, I'm sorry."

Stone knew nothing of this change in the law and she'd never hired a car before – she wasn't the first to be caught out she was told.

She could see where this was going to lead, argument would be pointless. A flea in the ear of her transport manager for not telling her might be helpful for the future.

The airport information desk was only a short distance away, there she asked for security. The man on the desk dialled a number and within a couple of minutes two armed police officers were at her side asking what the problem was, one was a sergeant.

"I'm really sorry to trouble you but I have a problem that I have to resolve with discretion," she addressed the sergeant. She produced her MI5 identity card that the officer scrutinised.

"How can we help miss?"

Stone explained the problem. She and the officers went over to the Europcar office. The sergeant went in and was only there for a short time. He remerged grinning. "All sorted," he said. Amazed and impressed she was given the keys to a hire car immediately.

It was tipping down with rain when she finally got underway in the little Renault Before leaving the office in London she had established what hotel Hammond had stayed in and rang them to reserve a room. It was still raining when she arrived at her destination – the hotel in Ballater.

Archie, the owner of the hotel was at the reception when she arrived, it was very quiet which suited her down to the ground.

Having introduced herself Archie carried her bag upstairs and showed her to her room, she glanced at her wristwatch – it was 6 pm. She unpacked her bag and had a wash and brush-up before going down to the bar; she was looking gorgeous in black jeans and a black top with a tan bomber jacket.

It was the first time she'd been to Scotland and was looking forward to seeing Balmoral; she was staying for two nights. Colonel Fergusson had agreed to see her at 11 o'clock in the morning.

The bar was empty apart from Archie who was serving.

"What can I get you miss?"

"A gin and tonic please, with ice and lemon. Is this a quiet time of year for you?"

"Far from it," he replied glancing at his watch. "Give it another half and hour and you'll see."

Passing Stone her drink he asked." Now, how can I help you?" He was a bit wary. Who was this woman who said she was a civil servant?

"I work for MI5 and I would like you to treat this matter with the utmost confidentiality." She produced a photograph from her bag and slid it across the bar. "I believe this gentleman stayed with you recently." It was an image of Hammond.

He put his spectacles on, they were on a chain around his neck, and looked at the image.

"Yes, he was a here for a few nights – why?"

"I can't answer that. What can you tell me about him and his visit?"

"Well, he seemed a nice fellow, very knowledgeable about fishing and shooting. He chatted to a lot of the guests and fitted in very well. When he wasn't biting his nails he was good company."

"Why was he here specifically?"

"I think he stayed here because of our proximity to the Balmoral Estate. He said he was researching the possibility of a McNab as a present for his father. I remember I gave him the factor's telephone number."

"Sorry, please forgive my ignorance but what's a McNab and what is a factor?"

"In sporting terms a McNab is a great achievement and there aren't many that have done it. Basically in a twenty-four hour period you have to shoot a grouse and a stag and catch a salmon. Balmoral is a great place to attempt it. I wouldn't mind the opportunity as a present I can tell you. A factor is an estate manager."

"Thanks. I'm going to see Colonel Fergusson tomorrow. Did Hammond meet anyone while he was here, maybe a stranger?"

"Not that I saw while he was in the hotel."

Just then a dozen or so men came into the bar, all wearing breeks and all with weathered faces. Apologising to Stone Archie broke off to serve them. A group of fisherwomen then arrived at the same time as Archie's assistant, it was getting busy as he'd predicted.

He rejoined Stone.

"I've just remembered; I did introduce your man to Jimmy James who looks after the Games Gathering ground at Braemar. I'll give you his number."

They carried on chatting as more and more anglers arrived. Archie had to concentrate on his customers and having given Stone James' number went back to serving. It was busy and very noisy; business was clearly good.

She was sitting in a corner at the end of a bar and was waiting to get another drink and to enquire about a table for her supper. A tall, good looking man approached her with a quizzical look. "Excuse me but is it Nat Stone?"

"It is, but do I know you?"

"Ah, it's the beard I guess, nobody seems to recognise me since I've grown it. Matt Rigby."

"Matt! God no I didn't recognise you at all, it's a good disguise. How long is it? I don't mean the beard but it must be eleven or twelve years, how are you?"

"I'm really well thanks and you look absolutely stunning."

"What happened to you after Uni, you seemed to drop off the planet?"

He laughed. "I've been in Africa until recently. What would you like to drink?"

"A gin and tonic please."

Archie arrived and got the drinks, as he delivered them Stone asked if there was a table for one available in the dining room. Before he could answer Matt insisted that she join him and his friends for dinner. "No arguing! We've got a lot to catch up on."

She laughed and accepted.

It was a very convivial evening between Nat and Matt. It ended at about three in the morning drinking whisky in front of a crackling log fire. Archie had left them a bottle before going to bed. Both vowed to continue their conversation the next evening before retiring to their rooms.

They'd been drinking a very good malt whisky renowned for its smoothness and purity, she was still surprised not to have a hangover in the morning. As a cover for her visit she told Matt and his friends she was a civil servant surveying the security installations at Balmoral.

"I've read the report that you compiled into Mr Hammond's recent visit and I would like to ask some questions if you don't mind."

She was with Colonel Fergusson, the factor.

"No, I don't mind at all, fire away."

"You said he was researching some sporting possibilities as a birthday present for his father."

"Correct."

"Did you believe him?"

"Yes, he seemed very plausible and was knowledgeable about field sports."

"Other than the sport issue did he ask you any other questions?"

Fergusson thought for a moment. He was always quite ponderous when he was thinking, thorough if you like.

"He did bring up the subject of security here while we were on the hill but his questions didn't ring any alarm bells – they seemed innocent enough."

"How did you leave the matter?"

"I am going to write to him when I receive some costings, probably tomorrow."

"Would you mind sending me a copy, preferably by email? What address are you writing to?"

"Yes I can send you a copy."

The address he gave was the same as that on Hammond's driving licence.

"What should I do if Hammond contacts me again?"

"Act normally and let me know."

She handed the Colonel her contact details.

Looking at the contents of the folder she said, "It says here that one of the ghillies saw him in his Land Rover from the hill, apparently he kept stopping and starting – any idea why he would do that?"

"No but I'll see if Gordon's about."

He picked up a two-way radio from his desk and called him, he was just driving into the yard at the back of the office as luck would have it. Fergusson asked him to come in.

"Gordon, this young lady is here about the visitor we had recently that you spied from the hill."

"Hello Gordon. When you spied this man what do you think he was doing?"

"Weel it seemed strange that he should keep stopping and starting and using his camera, the odd thing that drew my attention is he wasn't scanning the sky or the hills, where you might expect to see something, but the road and I couldn't work out why - he was always on a straight stretch."

"So what do you think he was up to?"

"Och, I couldna say."

She walked over to the wall map and asked Gordon to point out where the vehicle stopped and where he was, he marked the positions on her OS map.

After thanking the Colonel and Gordon she set off in the direction of Tomintoul retracing the route Hammond had taken. Stopping at the spots marked on her map she looked long and hard at the prospect in front of her, nothing untoward. She wished she'd had binoculars with her although, as an afterthought she wondered if they'd have been of any use, her eyesight was good.

Next she drove to Braemar where she was meeting Jimmy James at the Invercauld hotel. She'd rung him and made an appointment that morning. He had beer and she had a coffee but he couldn't add much to what she already knew other than he thought Hammond seemed genuine.

The day started wet but had gradually cleared up and was now sunny and warm as she drove around having a look at the stunning landscape of the Cairngorms. She would come back another time – wonderful biking country she thought to herself.

Chapter
9

Gazelle was sitting in the airport departure area drinking coffee while waiting for his flight to London. His mobile rang - a man said in Arabic 'Evacuate' - it was a prearranged code word. This meant something had gone wrong with the operation. Precautions had been discussed and a plan of action had been made.

He deleted the call from the phone's log and composed messages to Hammond and Gallagher's link men – 'LEAVE'. He looked at his watch, 1 pm. It would be 2 pm UK time that the link men received it – he pressed send. There was no doubt the link men would redirect the message immediately but Hammond wouldn't receive it until the appointed time for him to turn his phone on – 6 pm, Gallagher 6.45 pm - would he be in time with his warning he asked himself.

Hammond had left his Land Rover, not outside but near his house in Colchester and had taken the train to Liverpool Street; he was going to a party in London. He took the tube and decided to walk past his 'address' to collect the videos of his Scottish visit he'd requested, it was on the way to his destination.

Two things happened just as he was approaching the house. Firstly, his mobile bleeped, a text message, he took the wrong mobile from his pocket. He found the right one and read the text - LEAVE. As he was putting the mobile back into his pocket a red Ford came hurtling around the corner and came to an abrupt halt about fifty yards past the house. It was unmarked with two occupants; he was certain they were police – a close shave. He walked on.

Gallagher was just pulling into a service station on the M74 on his way back to Glasgow; he hadn't seen the need to go to his London 'address' so was unaware that the house was being watched. He needed fuel and a loo break. As he stopped by the pumps his mobile bleeped, his LEAVE text. He drove away from the pumps and parked in the very busy car park. After wiping the car interior down with his handkerchief he took his bag, left the keys and walked to the restaurant area. He called a cab which he took to continue his journey.

Stone loved living in Walthamstow market - she adored the ethnic diversity of the people living and working there. Beneath her flat was a shop selling Polish food and opposite a famous eel and pie shop. It was 7.30 in the morning and the stall holders were busy setting up; she was off to Norfolk to stay with her cousin and best friend, Fiona and meeting up with Jack Christmas, the Sandringham gamekeeper, to ask him about Gallagher's visit. The weather was, and was forecast to remain, beautiful for the next few days.

She wheeled the Norton from its lock-up in the High Street and it started first time with a roar; she hadn't had the opportunity to use it for a while. She wove her way through the traffic to the North Circular and then onto the M11, the road was getting busier and busier, people probably on the way to the coast on such a fine day.

Heading for the village of Great Massingham, about a dozen miles from Sandringham, she went through Brandon. The whole ensemble, the black bike, green leathers and white helmet made an eye-catching sight and heads turned, but it was impossible to distinguish the gender of the rider. Clear of the town she had the opportunity to open the bike up – the brute power, like the acceleration, was incredible. Watching out for cops and deer she wound the machine up to 140mph on one stretch through the edge of Thetford Forest – amazing. Next was Swaffham, then north under the big open skies and undulating countryside of West Norfolk.

Fiona and Nat's mothers were sisters. The formers mother was in a care home with dementia, her father disappeared years ago. Ever since the Stone family returned to the UK Nat had spent her summers in

Norfolk with Fiona who now ran her mother's small equestrian business – the two girls had become inseparable.

When they were 12 years old their friendship became firmly entrenched after they'd shared a terrifying (to them) experience.

On a fine day they went on a pic-nic with instructions from Fiona's mother to collect some blackberries. To get to the best blackberrying spot they had to cross a stream on a single plank bridge. The sun was hot and their pic-nic of strawberry jam sandwiches and lots of lemonade was delicious. They collected their belongings and the basket-full of berries they'd gathered and headed home. They got to the stream and, horror of horrors, there he was, standing on the bridge staring angrily at them – they were petrified. Fiona, a country girl, told Nat not to be afraid but to put her basket down and walk slowly to the hedge with her. As they reached the hedge the enormous, horned and bearded Billy goat went toward the baskets leaving the way clear for the girls to escape, they ran hell for leather to the farmhouse.

In tears they explained to Fiona's father what had happened, he suppressed his laugh and took the girls back to the scene of the crime – the only evidence left was a lemonade bottle, a plastic sandwich box and the chewed remains of their baskets.

******

Max Simmonds was the poster boy of the intelligence services. Tall, with black wavy hair and steely blue eyes he had a wonderful voice, some might say sexy, others mellifluous - he charmed everyone.

He knew he was attractive to women and was an incorrigible flirt. His latest conquest was Katrine, the forty year old ex-wife of the French ambassador. The only blemish to his countenance was a port-wine stain to his right temple. His father had the same birthmark even though it was not thought to be hereditary he was living proof that it was.

He'd reached the top of the tree in his chosen career but wasn't satisfied with his life. From a well to do background he lived in a fine house overlooking Wimbledon Common. His marriage, mainly because he was a philanderer, had developed into an open one – it seemed to suit both him and his wife Jane, she had her beau and he had his secret hide away where he could entertain a seemingly endless line of women - perfect he thought. They got together occasionally and all appeared normal, even to their son Tom who he was very close to.

The house in Cornwall, near St Mawes, was inherited by Jane and was in her name. Simmonds had inherited a legacy from an aged aunt of £250,000 and a stunning ex-gatekeeper's lodge in Regent's Park worth considerably more. It was a tiny one bedroom property but suited his purposes ideally. He inherited the cash and property three years before but never told his wife.

He was chairing the meeting at New Scotland Yard in Boswell's office, it was 7 am. Boswell, McLeod and Nat Stone were present; Maria Webley was taking the minutes.

"Nat, can we start with your report?"

"Yes sir. First I went to Balmoral and talked to the factor, a ghillie and the man that looks after the Highland Gathering showground. The ghillie thought Hammond was up to something but didn't know what. His boss the factor and the showground manager thought there was nothing unusual in Hammond's behaviour. I went over the same ground as him and the only thing I can think of was that he was surveying the land as a sniper might, but I have no evidence or experience of that.

"I had much the same response from the head gamekeeper at Sandringham –he didn't see anything unusual in Gallagher's enquiries."

It may seem to be a trivial amount of information but it's very important for any operative to get the whole picture and to try and understand the suspect's psychology.

"Thank you for that Nat, well done. Betine, have you heard of any plot against the Royals on the grapevine?"

"Nothing Max. We have had a whisper about an attack on infrastructure, but it is only a whisper. It's incredibly busy down at GCHQ, so much chatter but at the moment it's all rather vague."

"Okay. There has been no activity at either of the properties we've been watching. Our checks as to who pays the rents, council tax, utilities and the like reveal they're all paid by an off-shore company called Eagleton, registered in the Cayman Islands – we've come up against a brick wall with them. The property agents confirm that Eagleton pays the rent. We have a complete blank on Hamilton and Gallagher and we haven't found the two Land Rovers yet – these were paid for in cash and apart from the names in the V5C's we don't know who paid for them. The car dealer that Jim Tyson pulled in says it was Hammond and provided a copy receipt to him.

"So, apart from the fact that both vehicles were bought from the same dealer and they were both seen on Royal Estates what do we have?"

"Nothing it would seem," said Ned Boswell. "But it all points to the early stages of a plot in my opinion. In any case I'm going to step up our presence at Balmoral and Sandringham."

"Right, we will enter the two properties and see what, if anything, we find. At the same time let's step up the search for these individuals and their vehicles, I'll ask the police to do the latter and to help us with Hammond and Gallagher. Do we think it's the right time to go public?"

They were all weighing up the pros and cons. After a few moments pause they agreed to leave it a little longer.

Gazelle finally got home after delays to his flight, he was worried. He discovered, through a member of the Brotherhood working for the police, that the message EVACUATE meant the car dealer had been arrested and his records seized – the police were now looking for the two Land Rovers and Hammond and Gallagher.

He knew that he couldn't be connected to the dealer as he'd used an intermediary, nor was there a financial paper trail leading to him. He couldn't do anything about Hammond and Gallagher but, they were using false names - he was waiting to hear the outcome of his LEAVE text. What was niggling him was the incident at Heathrow. Nobody, until that incident, had a record of him, now the authorities will have a name and an image from his passport, it would be easy to find out where he lived and worked.

STAMFORD HILL was the text he sent to the two link men. They would pass this onto Gallagher and Hammond and all would know that it meant a meeting at 11 am at that Mosque on Friday.

Chapter
10

Gallagher's Land Rover was the first to be found, parked in the service area off the M74 there were no prints discovered, the vehicle was now with forensics.

As soon as Hammond had got back from his party on the last train he went home, got some wet-wipes, moved the Land Rover from where he'd parked it and wiped it down.

It took three days to find his vehicle down a track leading to allotments in Colchester, Essex - it was reported by a member of the public, it too was being examined by forensics. Essex police concluded that whoever left the Discovery where it was found must have had local knowledge because the allotments were so secluded, they were therefore going to concentrate their efforts to find the suspects in that area. All police had instructions not to apprehend any suspects but to inform MI5 of their whereabouts.

The problem was the images. The CCTV images were black and white and of poor quality - the systems at Balmoral, and other Royal estates, have since been updated to colour.

Police found the videos requested by Hammond and a letter with a quote from Fergusson at Balmoral but nothing else in the houses. Gallagher had never gone to his property. The videos could have come from anywhere and the prints lifted from the covers were unknown.

The forensics report on both Land Rovers revealed little – a single hair that was all but, it was a close match to a hair recovered from the back of the Jeep Cherokee used in the bomb attack on Glasgow airport in 2007. There was nothing on the Police DNA Database for the airport hair, but the one found on the passenger side floor of the Land Rover was a match to a soldier arrested and charged with attempted bodily harm three years ago, he was acquitted

Simmonds passed the report to Nat Stone for her to check out the soldier. It didn't take long for the MoD to get back to her – Patrick Seamus Gilligan, sergeant, 1st Battalion Royal Irish Regiment, reported missing presumed killed Helmand, Afghanistan 1st December 2015. The file was classified and would be sent over by courier.

Naturally Stone's eye was taken by the name Seamus and the surname beginning with G – a coincidence? Possibly - she rang Betine McLeod over at SIS to ask if she'd had any further thoughts on the image she thought she'd recognised – the one of Seamus Gallagher. Stone explained her request; security on the phone line was not a concern as it was a separate circuit operated by GCHQ.

"That's really interesting, as you know I spent time there. I'm looking at the image now but I still can't place him. Missing presumed dead you say? I need to see the image of Gilligan."

"It's on its way over from the MoD - as soon as it arrives I'll send you a copy."

The classified file with the photograph arrived. It went to Stone's boss; she didn't have the right security level. Comparing the photograph with the poor CCTV image taken in Norfolk it was annoyingly inconclusive. The one in the file was taken twelve years earlier. Stone sent it and height and build details to McLeod anyway in the hope that it jogged her memory. As a back-up she emailed the Estate manager at Sandringham attaching the image and asking if he could get Jack Christmas, the gamekeeper, to see if it was Seamus Gallagher.

The summary of the report was that Gilligan had been on special operations behind enemy lines in 2012 and was vaporised when he triggered an Improvised Explosive Device (IED). There was nothing left of him apart from a few scraps of clothing, there was no autopsy, no DNA testing on the clothing remnants and no witnesses. A copy of the order for him to carry out his mission was in the file. There were no known next of kin. Literally a dead-end she thought.

Sandringham got back to her pretty swiftly. Jack Christmas couldn't be sure if the image was Gallagher but he confirmed height and build to be about right. Everyone had said that Gallagher had green eyes and ginger hair but according to the MoD file Gilligan had grey eyes and fair hair.

Her conclusion was that if Gallagher and Gilligan were the same person the latter wasn't dead and the former dyed his hair and changed his eye colour – probably contact lenses. She was puzzled, she may well be wrong – what to do?

Chapter

11

Much to Gazelle's relief both Hammond and Gallagher, along with their link men, arrived at the Stamford Hill Mosque. He had been told of Gallagher's change of appearance and complimented him on it.

Gallagher had taken a taxi from the service area on the M74 to Glasgow airport where he hired a car to get home. He had several fake licences along with DVLA codes so he had no difficulty. As soon as he got home after the LEAVE text he set about removing the henna dye from his fair hair and the green contact lenses.

Hammond explained how he'd had such a close shave with the police. Gallagher said he hadn't been in any danger as he hadn't gone anywhere near the safe house.

"Right, down to business. Could I have your report on your visit to Scotland H?"

Hammond unfolded an OS map of the Balmoral area and then gave his report using the map as a reference. He thanked his link man for organising the videos that he'd been unable to collect, but felt that he had accumulated sufficient information to come to a conclusion without them.

"In summary I believe an assassination on the Balmoral Estate is possible but has little chance of success and, undoubtedly, the perpetrator would be captured or killed. Apart from the police the Estate employs around 100 people, many of whom are gamekeepers, ghillies or shepherds who work on the moors and mountains – the hills have eyes and I'm certain no activity escapes them.

"The approaches to the Estate by vehicle cannot be covered because they are so varied. There is no fixed-wing airfield nearby and the River Dee on the Estate is not navigable. There is a helicopter landing pad adjacent to the castle. There maybe the chance of using a missile to bring the helicopter down but, of course, there's no guarantee the target would be on board. I visited the Highland Gathering venue in Braemar and Crathie Church that is used by the Royal family but, in my opinion, neither offers the right opportunities.

"In my view the best chance will be when the target is fishing on the river. You see this woodland here," he said pointing with his finger on the map. "A sniper would have perfect cover in the trees and it's a good vantage point looking down on the river. At this point the target would be wading, probably chest deep, so they would, in effect, be stationery. Access to the woods at night should be easy, but the sniper may have to wait for maybe two or three days assuming the target does fish. Until we know the target that isn't possible to say. The fisherman would not be alone, one or two ghillies would be in the vicinity and they are in constant contact with the police and other staff by radio. Escape afterwards would be impossible."

"G, how did you get on?"

"I think it would be possible and with a chance of escape for the killer but, more research is needed and knowing who the target is to be is essential.

"Like Balmoral the Sandringham Estate covers a huge area, more than 20,000 acres and is mainly agricultural, villages are few and far between. That's not to say it's quiet.

"I understand that when the family is in residence the area crawls with armed police, most are easily visible as they drive about in immaculate, dark colour Land Rovers; others remain hidden around any venue that's being used.

"Additionally the estate employs at least nine gamekeepers who criss-cross the area from dawn to dusk. On top of that you have the farmers and walkers, it's a popular location for holiday-makers but I think some of this activity might be useful for our purpose.

"The two ideas that I have need to be worked up. Do we have access to a good sniper? They will need to be proficient up to 1,000 metres. As far as timing is concerned the operation could take place this summer with further research, or the other operation in the winter months.

"That's as far as I can go until I know the target, but I do think there's an opportunity for a successful hit."

"This is most interesting and encouraging G. I have noted your requirements and will let you have the answers in due course. Thank you both, I will be in touch."

Gazelle had to go abroad the next day, Toronto then to Cairo to have another meeting with the Brotherhood, this information will be a crucial topic.

******

His father's crude words were ringing in Simmonds' ear - 'never, ever poke the pay roll' – Stone was bent over in front of him picking up a file she'd dropped while lewd thoughts were running through his mind: an old cliché but he was old enough to be her father - that didn't bother him.

"I'm sorry to trouble you sir but I'm stuck. There seems to be a fifty-fifty chance that one of our suspects, Gallagher, is someone else who's supposed to be dead." She went through her thoughts.

"Have you looked through the Glasgow airport bombing file? You might find something there. Pay particular interest to forensics to see if there's any link to the soldier apart from the hair they found."

"Okay, I'll do that sir, thank you."

"I think under the circumstances I will increase your security level clearance and let you have the Gilligan file subject to the usual conditions – no copying, it stays in the office and you don't talk about the contents. If you go and see Maria, I'll tell her, and she'll get you to sign the paperwork and give you the file, you'll see some interesting stuff in there. Let me know how you get on."

Stone was over the moon, she felt she was making real progress and was grateful to her boss for this advancement.

She was aghast as she read the Gilligan file. Some of it had been redacted but the main point was that before he joined the army in 2006 he worked for what was then the Royal Ulster Constabulary and had infiltrated the IRA - he was an undercover cop, blimey she thought, this was mega. The file left her thinking if any of it was true – it would be impossible to verify. The link to Gilligan and Gallagher was so slim – just one hair and a prosecution would never stand up on that alone, even she knew that.

With that she turned to the Glasgow bombing file and began to read it, tome like as it was. There were finger print records in the file but as Gilligan was supposedly dead they couldn't be checked against his, the ones in his file didn't match either. She decided to make a time-line.

Gilligan was in the RUC 2004-2006 when he then joined the army, he was killed in 2012. The Glasgow bomb was June 2007 and, if that's who it was, was seen in Norfolk in April this year. That meant that Gilligan must have been in the army at the time of the bomb incident, she would have to check his whereabouts at the time with the MoD. Somehow she just knew that his whereabouts would be anywhere but Glasgow.

If Gilligan and Gallagher was the same person, then this was one very clever ruse that must involve high-up resources to be able to alter or fabricate these government files.

Deep in thought her mobile rang, it was Colchester police, they'd had a sighting of Hammond. Within twenty minutes she was on her way in a pool car with a young colleague called Callan. Simmonds told her to report only to him.

Chapter
12

She was a fast, competent driver and they got to Colchester without the 'blues and twos' in one hour and fifty minutes. Detective Inspector Harris was waiting to greet her in the reception of the police station – she produced her ID and introduced herself and Callan. They followed the DI into a briefing room where a uniformed WPC was waiting, everyone was introduced.

"I understand that you spotted the suspect WPC Hollis. Did you recognise him from the photograph that was circulated?"

"Yes."

"How tall would you think he is?"

"About 6 feet I'd say."

"When and where did you see him?"

The DI had ordered coffees that arrived at that moment, once these had been distributed the conversation continued. They walked over to a wall map of the town.

"I was patrolling here," she said pointing to the map, "When I saw him crossing the road and going into the Mosque just here. I parked up and waited and reported in. He never came out again and after half an hour I came back to the station."

"We've discreetly checked the building out and it has two entrances and he must have slipped out of the one at the back," said the DI.

"What time did you see him WPC?"

"At 10.55 this morning."

"I've stationed a plain clothes officer in the car park opposite the Mosque and another at the back, they will report in if the suspect comes back."

"He will - I'm certain, probably this afternoon for prayers. Is there somewhere here we can get some lunch while we're waiting?"

"Yes, I'll show you to the canteen and let you know if anything happens," said the DI.

While Callan was queuing for sandwiches Stone called her boss to give him an update.

"Understand that under no circumstances is the suspect to be detained, just keep a close watch. Do you have sufficient resources?"

"For the moment sir."

DI Harris joined them with a coffee and asked if there was anything else he could do.

"When we've finished our sandwiches could you direct us to where the Land Rover was found please?"

They went off in the DI's car to the allotments located down an unmade, unmarked lane off a smart road between two Victorian villas – strangely remote but it's easy to forget these rural towns are built around the countryside. Yes, you would need local knowledge to know that it's there. The DI's mobile rang – the suspect had just arrived at the Mosque in Priory Street, it was 3.50pm.

"Do you have any binoculars in the car sir?" asked Stone as they pulled into a far corner of the car park opposite the Mosque.

The DI reached to the glove box and took out a pair of police issue mini-binoculars and handed them to her, and then they waited. Stone was keeping her fingers crossed that the identification of the suspect was right, but she was apprehensive.

It was an hour before he reappeared and walked down Priory Street, a plain clothes officer got out of his car in the car park and followed. A clever radio system enabled the DI and his two plain clothes officers to communicate. As a woman on a bicycle went by Harris said that she was the second look-out. Looking through the binoculars Stone was certain this was the right suspect – she was excited.

The suspect was followed along the Lexden Road heading west and went into a property within a block of maisonettes. The white stuccoed art deco buildings lay back from the road behind a screen of Scot's pines.

The DI and his passengers cruised past trying to identify a good spot to keep a watch on the property. Even though the trees acted as a good cover, other than a villa opposite, there wasn't one. They would have to commandeer the property and set up a stake out. Harris contacted the police station and instigated checks on the occupant of the maisonette and put the commandeering in progress.

Stone contacted her boss to see if she should stay and wait for something to happen or return. He told her to come back to London.

It was quickly established the suspect's real name was Wolfe Dean and he'd lived at the property for three years, he had no criminal record. He owned an old red VW Golf GTI that was parked at the back of the maisonette. A tap was put on his telephone and a tracker on his car, a 24/7 watch was in place – nothing happened for forty-eight hours.

This was one of the better jobs the two CID officers had been on, surveillance is boring at the best of times but the woman that owned the house was charming. To avoid comings and goings she put them up as well as supplying delicious food. No smoking in the house, but they were welcome to do so in the back garden which wasn't overlooked.

It was just before 11 am. One was watching the house, the other wearing earphones was waiting for any phone calls when the suspect came out of the building opposite. Alarm bells rang in their heads, he was carrying two aluminium cases and had a black wrapped package about three feet long over his shoulder. He disappeared to the back of the property and then re-emerged in his car. The officer on look-out immediately rang DI Harris and told him the suspect was on the move and had the two cases and a package.

Two things happened next, a pursuit car was instructed to follow the VW at a distance using the tracking device and an armed response vehicle was dispatched as well, just in case. Harris then called Max Simmonds to advise him that the suspect was on the move.

The VW was followed to Mersea Island, not far from Colchester. It stopped near a church where it looked like a wedding was about to take place. The driver was sitting in the car watching the growing crowd, as they moved into the church the bride arrived, when she had gone in he decanted the cases and the package and proceeded to unpack them and set up a camera on a tripod outside the church entrance.

Stone had got back to the office to a message from the MoD – Gilligan had been in hospital in Kabul with a broken foot at the time of the Glasgow bombing – surprise, surprise she thought.

So, they had one of the suspects, Dean aka Hammond, although all he had done was go to Balmoral and had been in possession of a vehicle that had come from a spurious source – not much. As far as the other suspect was concerned, Gilligan/Gallagher she didn't have a clue.

Chapter

13

Again the meeting was at Thames House, the usual team were present – the three heads and the secretary. The lead topic was the one that Stone had been working on, it had been given a name – operation Jonah.

Simmonds liked to give his young protégés their head, he encouraged them to speak their mind and not hold back. He'd witnessed some brilliant youngsters in action; he liked their young, agile minds and determination. He called Stone into the room.

"What have you got for us Nat?"

"As you know sir we have tracked down Hammond, his real name is Wolfe Dean and he lives in Colchester. He's under twenty-four seven surveillance by the local CID; as yet he hasn't led us anywhere. We have carried out all the usual checks but we have nothing on him, there are no irregularities with his finances.

"With regard to Gallagher, I'm still not sure what we're dealing with there. The only thing linking him to the dead soldier, Gilligan, is a near, and I must emphasise near, DNA match on a single hair. My gut feeling is that they are one and the same person but, as yet, there's nothing to substantiate this.

"As the vehicles came from the same source Gallagher and Hammond must be working together and clearly, as they were both seen on Royal Estates, they must be plotting against members of the Royal family.

"Both Land Rovers were abandoned at around the same time. The suspects must have been tipped off that the authorities were interested in them. No one, other than us, knew of the interrogation of the car dealer and the group that were rounded up therefore, the tip-off must have either come from within or, it was the dealer which I think is unlikely: to my mind that means a well organised force is behind this plot."

"Very good," said Simmonds, "what do you propose?"

"Gallagher's vehicle was found at the Abington northbound service area on the M74. I'm going to suggest he lives in Scotland and I propose we circulate the images of both Gallagher and Gilligan to the Scottish police and say we are looking for two men. If we have no luck there I'm certain Hammond will lead us to him in due course. I think that we shouldn't lose sight of the fact this might just be some sort of decoy.

"Could I ask a question of the meeting sir?"

"Of course, fire away."

"Who do you all think is behind this – is it the IRA?"

The three heads looked at each other, Betine McLeod spoke first.

"I can see where you're coming from Nat, you're thinking about Gilligan and his connection to Northern Ireland. Because of the nationality of the group that Jim Tyson rounded up, including the car dealer, I'm more inclined to think that ISIL or Al Qaeda are behind it - clever of them to use white Brits for their reconnaissance. If it hadn't been for the chance questioning of the car dealer we'd have had no ideas at all."

"Go careful with Police Scotland when you contact them Nat, they've recently reorganised and there have been problems," said Simmonds. "If Betine is right this is a new terrorist cell that we have no intelligence on. At the moment Hammond is key in all this so it's essential we do not lose him. Nat, make sure Colchester police have sufficient resources to keep tabs on him. Be careful how you word that as if you mention more money they'll grab it with both hands and you'll probably get nothing in return.

"If we've finished with Jonah for the moment I'll let Nat get on," he looked around the table and the other heads agreed."

"Thank you Nat, we're very impressed, keep up the good work."

She was grinning ear to ear as she left the room.

******

Gilligan, using one of his many pseudonyms, lived in a remote part of Argyll about 40 minutes from Oban. His partner, Trevor, waved as he drove up the track in the hire car to the small idyllic white painted cottage. Trevor, from south London always greeted him in a bad Irish accent as Paddy, he was a painter and quite successful too.

Trevor knew most of Gilligan's secrets but not all. Strangely, instead of the strongly built Gilligan who looked so Alpha male, it was weedy looking Trevor who was the dominant partner. They'd been together since Gilligan had left the army due to ill health, so he told Trevor.

They lived a strange existence, Gilligan never told Trevor what he did for a living or where he'd been and Trevor knew better than to ask as he would only get short shrift. Both enjoyed a love of cooking and after provisions had been unloaded from Gilligan's car Trevor set about preparing supper.

About as isolated as you can get on the mainland the cottage had no electricity or mains water; that came from a nearby burn. The only nod to modernity was a diesel generator, located well away from the cottage, used mainly for operating a shower, heating and cooking were from a wood burning range – there was plenty of timber in the grounds. There was no radio reception, no phone, no internet and mobiles didn't work.

Rarely did they go anywhere together. In the cottage they read, cooked, played cards or board games and listened to the battery operated CD player, when the generator was going they used the power from that. They talked a lot on a vast range of subjects, as a fly on the wall it would have been fascinating especially so as neither of them had had any education to speak of.

It must have been a week later that Gilligan drove to Oban to re-provision. It was a nice morning, sunny but with a cold wind from the north-west. As he cleared the lonely glen the car radio suddenly burst into life, because of the terrain there wasn't a signal until that point. Just as he was pulling into Tesco's car park the BBC news came on, he parked up to listen to it.

He was staggered when he heard the third item – how the hell had they got on to him was what he asked himself. Police would like to interview two men, Gilligan and Gallagher about an incident in Norfolk said the reporter. He was amused that they'd used both names; surely they must know they are one and the same, maybe they didn't he told himself.

Was Gazelle back? Did he know about this? He needed to text his link man with these questions.

He considered his appearance before getting out of the car. Unshaven for over a week, wearing a dark blue Guernsey and shabby jeans he looked perfectly normal and fitted in with those around him. The supermarket was as busy as ever with holidaymakers swelling the crowd.

Studying the front pages on the news-stand in the foyer he couldn't see the story. He picked up a copy of the Oban Times and leafed through it, there it was on page four with two images of him, fortunately they were both black and white. The one of Gallagher was fuzzy and the army one was old and he thought bore little resemblance, he sighed with relief and got his shopping. He decided to keep the beard.

After his final stop to get some diesel he went to the cottage, his mobile bleeped as he was leaving the garage, it was a text - Not Back. Twice the story was repeated on the radio on his way back before he lost the signal. He didn't mention it; it wouldn't have meant anything to Trevor anyway.

In fact Gazelle, who was in Toronto, had picked up the story on-line. Having considered the low quality images and the small amount of information given in the article he'd read he decided there was little or no risk to the project. However, he was concerned that the authorities had two different images of Gallagher, what did they really know about him? He didn't know that Hammond was under observation.

Nervous about the UK authorities he needed to come up with a different meeting venue when he returned just in case anyone was being followed.

Airport security was incredibly tight. An Air Egypt aircraft had been brought down by a bomb over the sea near Alexandria just a few days before, as a consequence Gazelle had a rotten trip to Canada, stopped and questioned three times at Heathrow and twice in Toronto he was feeling paranoiac about his ethnicity. Tomorrow he was off to Cairo.

Stone had put her plan in place with Police Scotland and Hammond was under surveillance; all she could do now was to wait for something to happen. It was 7.30 pm and just as she was packing up to go home her mobile rang.

"Hello Nat, its Matt Rigby. I was wondering if you would like to meet up for a meal so we can continue where we left off in Scotland – what do you think"

Chapter
14

The week had gone by with little activity on operation Jonah. No sign of Gallagher/Gilligan. Hammond, apart from his regular visits to his Mosque for prayers, had been busy with his photography keeping his watchers on their toes to no avail.

Stone was due to have lunch with Matt Rigby today. They were going to meet in the country if it was a fine day, if not then in town. It was sunny and hot so she decided to use the bike, it needed an airing and she felt like showing off.

In the end she decided on the Bell and Crown, a riverside inn at Strand on the Green, they would meet there at 12.30. She was fashionably late and secretly hoping he would be at a table outside as she pulled up. He was, as this vision in green stopped outside the pub. Not realising it was her until she removed her helmet he thought they were strange colour leathers for a bloke to be wearing – probably an Italian he'd thought.

She stripped off to a white T shirt and jeans, putting her leathers and helmet on a chair, it was hot. Carrying on their animated conversation from where they'd left off they were on the dessert course of an indifferent meal when her mobile rang, she glanced at the screen; it was Simmonds.

"Sorry, please excuse me a moment, it's my boss." She didn't wait for an answer but walked to the kerb answering as she went.

There had been a tentative sighting of Gallagher/Gilligan. He'd been stopped on a traffic check in Scotland driving a hire car, his papers were in order. The driver's name was David Anderson. The officer wasn't one hundred per cent sure, but the bearded driver was of a similar height and build as the suspect, he had fair hair and grey eyes and looked a bit like the images he had with him in his police car.

The hire car had been subjected to a routine search as the route was the only one into Argyll from the south, guns and drugs were known to be brought into the area this way, nothing was found and the driver was sent on his way. The hire company at Glasgow airport was contacted and confirmed the name of the driver, but the police officer had a gut feeling about him. Police Scotland asked MI5 to check out the London address in the driver's licence, it was false, the licence was a fake.

"I'm really sorry Matt but it's urgent, I have to go back to the office. It's a shame as I was really enjoying myself. Can we try again soon? Let me know when you can manage it" She put on her riding kit, kissed him on the cheek and was away at speed.

He was not best pleased but didn't show it. Much as he'd tried to find out he really didn't know what her work was, this intrigued him and he wouldn't give up on her just yet, he liked her.

The thundering of the motorbike's powerful engine reverberated around the underground car park at Thames House as she rode down the ramp. She was so excited she ran to her office to find out what was happening.

"The car hasn't been returned to the airport yet," said Simmonds. "The police are checking flight manifests at the moment and they've increased security there and at Queen Street station in Glasgow. Don't get overexcited yet Nat, it's only one sighting and not one hundred per cent certain."

Gallagher could have kicked himself. Why the hell did he go that way, he'd been stopped before in exactly the same place just outside

Inverary, stupid, stupid, stupid! Tyndrum took longer but he'd never seen police on that route.

A change of plan was needed. Part of the hire company package was that he could return the car to any airport in Scotland; he decided to go to Inverness and fly to London from there. He pulled over and called the airport to see if he could get a seat on the next London flight - nothing until tomorrow.

He thought for a moment, he'd take the train to Euston - Arrocher station was just down the road. After parking the car in a secluded corner he entered the station and enquired as to when the next train was – he was in luck, a two hour wait. He went back to the car, wiped it down as much as possible, got his bag and went for something to eat while waiting for the train.

The day before he'd gone to Oban for provisions, he received a text from his link man as he drove in. Saturday – Greenwich pier – 1000. It was now Wednesday. Hammond had received a similar message. Saturday - Charing Cross pier - 0930.

It was more like winter than early summer in London, grey, cold and raining. Gallagher/Gilligan had stayed the night in Greenwich in a bed and breakfast, he thought it a miserable dump and decided to forgo breakfast; instead he had a good fry-up near the pier.

Hammond, with two plain clothes police in tow caught the 0700 train from Colchester to Liverpool Street. CID had asked London colleagues to have two men waiting at Liverpool Street to help with the tailing of Hammond. They were relieved by the London guys as Hammond set off. He hailed a cab which is where it began to get tricky; the two following did the same.

The cab pulled up along the Embankment near Charing Cross pier beside a coffee stand and Hammond got out.

Both he and Gallagher/Gilligan had been to Jihadi training camps and had been instructed in the art of following and being followed, Gallagher was an old hand.

Hammond ordered a coffee and as he did so he saw the cab that was behind his stopped a couple of hundred yards down the road, two men got out, crossed the road and stood around – it was obvious who they were, it was if they had blue flashing lights on their heads.

Just before 0930 he walked to the pier, it was high tide and there were a few boats there, the man on the stern of a small blue and white river cruiser hailed him. He boarded the boat and was sent down in to the cabin where Gazelle was waiting for him. The boat, stolen from a marina that morning, cast off immediately and moved downstream, there was nothing the police could do. Hammond now knew for certain they were onto him.

Crestfallen, the two London coppers called their colleagues from Colchester to say they'd lost the suspect. They also called the Marine Policing Unit at their Wapping base giving them a description of the cruiser and told them not to detain the boat but report its whereabouts if seen.

"Bugger, bugger, bugger! Back to square one and no nearer to catching the other one, sod it!" Tactfully, Stone who was with Simmonds kept quiet.

The journey to Greenwich was choppy and the rain was lashing down now, neither Gazelle or Hammond spoke. There were about thirty people on the pier waiting for various forms of river transport; among them were Gallagher and the two link men.

They continued downstream, it was very cramped in the cabin with five men plus, Ahmed (Gazelle's cousin) the skipper; the windows were steaming up. Gazelle started by debriefing Hammond and Gallagher. Addressing them both he asked how the men thought the authorities had got onto them – neither of them had an answer; both said they had been extremely careful. Gazelle didn't seem too stressed but said that it was inevitable given the heightened state of security everywhere.

He reminded all concerned that no one had done anything wrong to date. The authorities would be unable to prove a case of planning a terrorist act – they had no evidence.

Nobody on board noticed the navy-blue and white police launch sitting in Bow Creek, with its engines idling, observing the river traffic. The three man crew were on the look out for smugglers after receiving a tip-off. The officer sitting at the helm took the radio call about the river cruiser just as it went by. Immediately a call went shore-side and an unmarked patrol car was put into discreet pursuit alongside the river on the Woolwich Road.

Gazelle was a wise old owl; he'd put considerable planning into this meeting. Making various assumptions he felt it best to believe that one or all of his core team were being followed so he set out to confuse the authorities and, at the same time, move his project forward. He was certain they would not want to reveal themselves at this stage in case their suspects were frightened off.

They continued downstream with the tide now slack. Moving toward the shore Ahmed dropped anchor, shut off the engine and the meeting resumed with Ahmed acting as look-out.

"The committee of the Brotherhood was very impressed with your research," said Gazelle looking at Hammond and Gallagher. "They feel that the potential of a successful outcome lies with the Norfolk plan and would like that idea developed and that you two should work together to do that, your link men will assist.

"I need to know what you require to take the project forward. Here is a list of three trained snipers along with their CV's as you requested. You will of course need a weapon, but I presume the type will be dictated by the user."

Gallagher responded. "I will need some aerial photographs of the Sandringham estate including the marshes around Wolferton and of Anmer Hall. He put his OS map on the small cabin table and pointed to the specific areas, Gazelle wrote down the map references. Is there likely to be information on the family's movements in Norfolk?"

"The photographs will not be a problem. As for the family's movements I will try."

Simmonds was confused but saw this, through the eyes of a chess player like Gazelle, as part of the game. He was receiving varied radio reports about the boat but it was proving difficult to pin its location down as it went in and out of the view of the patrol car trying to follow it, at the moment it was out of sight. At least it had given him the chance to put a command structure in place.

He was in overall command; then Inspector Gibson of the Met, then CID Colchester. Simmonds ordered plain clothes officers to the two piers already used by the boat - two at each with instructions to follow the suspects if seen. He ordered another pursuit car on the other side of the river and look-outs on Tower Bridge all reporting to Gibson and then him to Simmonds. There was pressure to use a helicopter but he resisted.

Gazelle continued. "Now onto the most important issue, the target. After much deliberation the committee has decided on Prince William, the Duke of Cambridge for maximum impact on the degenerate UK, the younger generation in particular."

There was near silence on board the rocking boat, the only sound was the wavelets slapping against the hull.

There followed further conversation before the anchor was weighed. They set off for Greenwich pier, it was still pouring down with rain.

Quite a crowd was gathered on the pier, many with umbrellas. Among them were two plain clothes officers with instructions to photograph anyone who got off the cruiser and to follow them – easier said than done.

The first problem they were confronted with was that two men got off and each went in a different direction, furthermore it was obvious there were more people aboard, but they couldn't be seen clearly because of the misted up windows. They decided to wait to see and photograph who else got off the boat. The cruiser sat there with engine idling for at least two minutes before going off upstream – no one else got off – all part of Gazelle's detailed plan. The two men who went off were the link men.

Exactly the same performance was played out at Charing Cross pier. This time Ahmed and Hammond alighted and went in different directions. The latter was recognised and followed; as before, the other officer waited to see who else got off – no one. The boat moved off with Gallagher and Gazelle still heading upstream. They continued, without being clearly observed to Albert Bridge where they alighted and split up. Gazelle got straight into a waiting car and Gallagher caught a cab. Of course neither of them was photographed.

Someone, a male, waiting at the pier took control of the cruiser and headed back downstream. Passing the police launch going the other way it was only partly observed on its way to the river Lea where it turned upstream. On a quiet stretch of that river overhung with trees it was moored by the tow path, an incendiary device was ignited and the driver simply walked off across Hackney Marshes. The burnt out remains were found later that day - all forensics were destroyed in the fire. Simmonds was frustrated, all that effort and no result, although the photographs might reveal something.

The weather and poor light meant the images were next too useless and no one, apart from Hammond, was known to the authorities.

Chapter
`15

It had been agreed that Hammond's role hereon in would be one of a decoy as he was being followed. He would be notified of Gallagher's intentions and would draw his followers in the opposite direction.

With his beard, natural hair and eye colour Gallagher felt confident enough that he wouldn't be recognised. After hiring a car he went back to Norfolk and booked into a hotel in King's Lynn – Hammond drove to Windsor.

Stone, in the office, kept in touch via a steady stream of radio messages detailing his movements. Apparently he walked around the town, had a protracted lunch and drove back to Colchester. This was pointless she was thinking – a waste of resources and she told her boss just that – he agreed and everyone was told to stand down.

Gallagher was keen to do another recce of the area, in particular the Wash. After investigation he found there were no boat hire or river trips available in King's Lynn – he had to go to Brancaster, about half an hour away, to charter a boat. When he got there the boat was out but he got a mobile number from a board outside the office.

Heading south from Brancaster he went through the village of Bircham, a few miles down the road was the Anmer crossroads on the north-eastern corner of the Anmer estate. There was a crowd at the remote junction with vehicles almost blocking the lane. He thought he knew what they were doing, bird watchers – Twitchers, as before a number were wearing camouflage jackets, some with peaked caps.

He stopped and asked, he was right; sightings of a sea eagle had been called in. Apparently it's not rare but enthusiasts will travel a long way to see one. This was the second time he'd come across twitchers. The encounter reinforced an idea already in his head.

Continuing along the northern side of the estate what was noticeable, only by their absence, were the police Land Rovers, this could only mean the family were not in residence. He had another look at the wood not shown on his OS map and again gauged the distances from the wood to the Hall. He went back to his hotel and settled down to read the three sniper's CVs he had concealed in his hold-all, before it was time to eat.

Stone was due a bit of leave and there was a lull in operation Jonah. She decided to go and stay with Fiona for a few days, the weather was glorious and she could use the bike. On the way up to Great Massingham she'd reflected on her job and how much she loved it. Never again would she do 9 to 5; it never said so in her contract but in effect she was on call 24/7. It was unpredictable, a bit the like British weather she would tell friends, and she adored that.

Met in the yard by Bobby, Fiona's adorable terrier, he rushed over and made a big fuss. Fiona was just finishing off mucking out the stables, she'd finish this around 11am and most of the rest of the day was hers.

The weather next morning wasn't so nice and it was overcast. Fiona suggested that once she'd finished in the stables they should go in the car to Sandringham for a walk with Bobby – the azaleas and rhododendrons would be in flower.

"Would you like to see where Prince William and Kate live," asked Fiona. "It's just up here."

She turned off the main road into a narrow lane that ran down one side of the estate.

"You can't see a lot I'm afraid because they've screened it from the road, but it's down there on the right."

Stone was straining her neck to see when Fiona slammed on the brakes, a car was coming in the opposite direction and the lane was too narrow for them to pass. There was a stand-off for a moment then Fiona reversed about 100 yards and pulled in a field entrance. Stone was looking hard at the other driver, a bearded man. He thanked Fiona with a wave as he passed.

I think that's our missing man she said to herself – Gallagher aka Gilligan. At the same time, she grabbed a pen from her bag and scribbled the registration number on her hand.

"Can we stop here Fiona? I need to make an urgent call if I have a signal." She did but it was weak.

"I'm up in Norfolk sir, very near Anmer and I think I've just seen our prime suspect in a car. She gave Simmonds the registration number. "It's a green Ford. What do you want me to do?"

"Sit tight. Let me get the info on the car and I'll get straight back to you."

Sensing Stone was embarrassed Fiona told her not to worry, she didn't mind. She went off for a walk down the lane with Bobby while they were waiting for the call.

At last her mobile rang but the signal was poor, it cut out straight away. Fortunately, Fiona was coming back to the car and she took them to a place by Sandringham where there was a strong signal – the phone bleeped immediately – a text message.

The vehicle is a hire car on a stolen licence in the name of Mark Lawrence. Local police have been asked to apprehend because of the stolen licence, but not to mention Jonah. Will advise further. Simmonds.

Before leaving for Norfolk she had read Gilligan's file for the umpteenth time. There were so many words but so little told that she decided the whole thing was a charade, a construct but why and, more importantly, by whom.

They went to the woods with Bobby and carried on with their intended walk. It was getting on for time for Fiona to get back and deal with the horses. After getting some fish for supper they returned to Great Massingham.

It was a fine morning and while Fiona was dealing with horses she was having breakfast when her mobile rang – it was Simmonds.

"Good morning Nat. Your man has just been arrested on a stolen licence charge and I'd like you to go to King's Lynn police station and sit in on the questioning please. Report back to me."

"Okay sir, I'm on my way."

After getting directions from Fiona she fired up the bike and roared off at high speed along the wide, gently winding country road, it was exhilarating.

When she got to the police station an Inspector Davidson took her aside. Simmonds had spoken to him.

Gallagher had been stopped on the Hunstanton Road His licence was checked by radio and found to be stolen two years ago. He and the car had been brought back to the police station. The hire company confirmed that it was their vehicle, hired to a Mark Lawrenson, the name on the licence. The police didn't know where he was staying or what he was doing in the area. Neither did they know he'd been to Brancaster to discuss boat charter.

"I'm in a quandary with this man. We searched him for a weapon or drugs without result. All he had on him was a bundle of cash - £2,650 and a mobile - the call log had been deleted. He is saying nothing at all other than admitting his licence is stolen – bought it in a pub in London, and he's of no fixed abode. If I charge him it'll go to the magistrate's court and he'll get a fine that's all. What do you want me to do?"

"What would you charge him with?"

"Misrepresentation – hiring a vehicle using a false name and address; driving without a current driving licence and being in possession of a stolen driving licence – all minor offences and I certainly haven't got room or the resources to lock him up. He's declined a solicitor."

"Are you allowed to fingerprint and photograph him and take a DNA sample?"

"Yes I can, but only if I charge him, but even that's iffy."

Stone was thinking furiously. They wouldn't be able to keep him in custody on such charges, he would be released on his own bail and would obviously do a runner; there wouldn't be time to get the DNA results. They didn't even have proof of a name.

They might be able to hold him on suspicion of terrorism but, that would reveal their real motive. She rang Simmonds to see what he thought.

"Charge him with the offences you listed, take images, fingerprints and a DNA sample and release him. If he's our guy we've got a lot more than we had and we'll catch up with him later."

"Okay sir."

Gallagher seemed remarkably tolerant when charged and submitted to photography, fingerprints and a DNA swab, he was nonchalant. His bail was set at £250 which he paid in cash and he was told to surrender himself at the police station in fourteen days, they couldn't confiscate his passport as he didn't have one on him. He was released.

After walking back to his hotel to collect his bag he caught a cab to the railway station to take a train to King's Cross. The train wasn't very busy; he checked the false compartment in his holdall to make certain the tools of his trade were there: a 9mm revolver, two ammunition clips, three spare passports and two more driving licences along with the three CVs and a bundle of cash in Sterling and Euros.

Irina Kowlowski, ex-major in the Russian army. He was re-reading one of the sniper's CVs – he liked the idea of using a woman – the authorities wouldn't expect that. As you might expect the CV was short. She'd graduated with distinction at the Moscow sniper training centre and had worked in a number of theatres of war, most recently Syria – being a woman had not been a handicap. After leaving the army she went freelance – a gun for hire. There weren't too many career opportunities for an ex-sniper.

There was no photograph in the file - killers don't like to advertise themselves. No matter, Gallagher's experiences of female Russian military personnel was that they tended to be blond, blue eyes, tall and built like a T20 battle tank!

Her favoured weapon was a Drugunov SVD-1 rifle. Adapted to increase range, a relatively old-fashioned but deadly tool in the right hands – it was his favourite too.

He'd asked his link man for two things. Firstly, to fix an urgent meeting with Gazelle and secondly, to fix a meeting with the Russian sniper – he was waiting to hear back. She could be anywhere but he was gambling on London. Reflecting on his encounter with the police he felt he should remove the beard and add a touch of black dye to his hair.

He found a small B&B in the back streets of King's Cross and having purchased some short term hair dye and a good razor he set about his cosmetics – shaving off his established beard was painful - he wished he'd gone to a barber.

Chapter
16

His mobile bleeped, it was 2am, a text message telling him to meet Gazelle on a bus at 12 noon that day.

The bus wasn't crowded and they managed to get a seat upstairs at the back, the CCTV camera seemed to be pointing straight at them.

"I've selected the Russian woman as the sniper and I'm trying to meet up with her. How much can I tell her?"

"I know she will be back in London tomorrow. Don't tell her the target or the location for the moment, leave that to me. Any talk of the fee you should also leave to me. How is your plan progressing?"

"I should be ready to put my proposals in front of you soon. There are going to be some considerable expenses involved. Will you be able to source and purchase the weapon the sniper will require, or do you wish me to do that?"

"I will deal with that. What else?"

"The main item will be a three-man Hovercraft which will cost in the region of £10-15,000. It may be possible to hire one but I'm worried about the paper trail. We will also need an off road motorbike and a car – these can be stolen and used with false plates."

"A Hovercraft? How interesting." He raised an eyebrow.

"Yes, and I will need my link man or Hammond to take some training, once completed they should buy the craft."

"Okay. Anything else?"

"Not for the moment, apart from my expenses to date. They are for train fares, car hire and accommodation." He handed over the receipts.

Gazelle had a waist-band wallet. He checked the totals and removed a bundle of notes; he counted off £620 and gave it to Gallagher.

"When do you expect to have the aerial photographs that I need?"

"That should be tomorrow. If you write down the address of where you're staying they will be delivered to you."

Today's meeting was held in Ned Boswell's office at New Scotland Yard. The usual heads were there as well as Nat Stone; the latter was encouraged to summarise operation Jonah. The forensic report on Gallagher's samples taken at King's Lynn police station confirmed that his DNA matched the hair found in the Land Rover 100% - no surprise there. However, there was only a 50/50 match to the hair found at the Glasgow bomb scene; the lab felt the DNA on that hair had deteriorated over time.

Betine McLeod was sitting there with a vacant expression on her face, on another planet. Suddenly, interrupting Stone she exclaimed "Got the bugger!"

Everyone looked at her wondering what the hell she was on about.

"Well, nearly," she continued. "I know where I met this Gallagher/Gilligan character, we were introduced but I don't remember his name, he wasn't in uniform but wearing a suit. It was at a function, a small conference, being held by the Surgeon General at our embassy in Kabul. There was great concern about the number of throat and head wounds to our soldiers and a small number of leading specialist ENT surgeons were there to see if improvements to treatment could be found."

"Good," said Simmonds. "Can we get a guest list of all those present?"

"I'll try, but I know the embassy was fire-bombed shortly after the conference. There might even be some photographs; I know the embassy snapper was there."

The aerial photographs Gallagher had requested were delivered to his hotel as promised. While he was studying them he received a text message telling him to meet the Russian at a pub in Soho – The Lion's Head at 2pm.

Soho was very busy and the pub was crowded and noisy, not Gallagher's scene at all. He scanned the throng and in the corner by the bar he spotted a tall blonde, whoever came up with the idea of a sensitive meeting here needed shooting he thought. Eventually they made eye contact and he gestured to her to come over, she battled her way through the crowd and did.

He mouthed. "Are you Irina?"

She mouthed back. "Yes. Are you Seamus?"

"Yes, let's get out of here."

He led her down a side street without talking and went into an Italian coffee house finding a quite table in the corner. Tall, blonde and blue eyes were spot on - but she was anything but a battle tank. Beautiful and elegant she looked like a glamour model; he thought it a shame he wasn't sexually orientated that way. She couldn't be a killer - could she?

She'd never worked in England before and she was keen to learn about this potential assignment. Much to Gallagher's relief there was no chit-chat, straight down to business.

"Can you tell me who the target is?"

"Not at this stage."

"Can you tell me the location?"

"It's rural rather than urban – in the countryside."

She had an excellent understanding of English and she spoke it quite well too.

"Is this a summer or winter project?"

"It could be either but we are favouring summer."

"Is it in the UK?"

"Yes."

"What is the risk element?"

100

"We feel there is an 80% chance of total success."

Their coffee arrived and the conversation ceased whilst they drank.

"You know from my CV what my preferred weapon is – can you provide that?"

"Yes."

"Who do I discuss my fee with and assuming I accept when will I have details of the plan?"

"Both of those will be dealt with in due course but, before that can happen I need a demonstration of your ability as a sniper. Do you have any suggestions as to where you might do that?"

She thought for a moment.

"I do work for the Russian government and I might be able to use their underground shooting range at the embassy in Kensington Palace Gardens, but this will cost extra on my fee."

"Over what distance can you shoot?"

"It's only 500 metres but enough to give you an idea of my ability. Also I would need to zero the scope on the rifle there before the mission."

"When could this be arranged? You should know I will need to be there."

"I will have to enquire, but I'm not sure you will be allowed."

"Okay, let me know when and how much. Text me only on this number, do not call me." He wrote the number down and passed it to her.

Betine McLeod was excited when she rang Simmonds, it sounded in her voice.

"I was right - the written records of the guest list were destroyed in the fire. But, I do have five photographs of the event and some names. If you're free, I'll come over."

Ned Boswell wasn't around but he tracked down Nat Stone, she was with him when McLeod arrived. She spread the images on the table along with a key to the figures where known.

The five 10" x 8" images were all inscribed in white with a chinagraph number corresponding with the key.

McLeod explained. "This group of four is Daniel Long, Becky Thomas, me and Phil Gregory. Long is a surgeon at St Thomas', Thomas worked at the embassy and Gregory is an American, I'm waiting for his credentials to come back."

The next image showed a group of nine. The Surgeon General, the four in the previous image, Sheik Mohammed, two unknowns, one a woman, and someone called Brown. "That's him," she said pointing at Brown.

Simmonds and Stone looked closely at the image and agreed, it was Gallagher/Gilligan.

"Now, I've checked with the Royal College of Surgeons and all are bona fide, they are Fellows of the college; that is apart from the American which I am awaiting confirmation on, and Brown.

"Interestingly, the Sheikh was questioned and searched at Heathrow a few weeks ago, he was clean but the border guard was suspicious, he was tagged on the data base. We alerted our guys in Cairo, where he was flying to. The agent lost him for most of the time he was there. The Egyptians had nothing on him."

The rest of the images were a mixture of the previous individuals with one exception - that was Brown and the Sheikh alone in conversation. They probably didn't know they were being photographed.

Chapter

17

"What does this mean?" Simmonds asked. "Do we have a third man in this plot? "Who is this Sheikh Abdul Mohammed? Nat, I want you to get onto this, find out everything there is to know about this guy. Get Callan to work with you."

Starting with the Royal College of Surgeons she went over to Lincoln's Inn Fields. She had to produce her ID before they would give any information about the Sheikh, but his contact details were at a private clinic in Cairo, they had no details for London.

As usual for the younger generation she went onto a Google search, not a thing – strange. Then she tried Linked In, the same, nothing; then Facebook and other social media – this is going to be a slog she told herself, she called Callan in and they split the workload – they mustn't spook the suspect.

Gallagher got back to his hotel and studied the aerial photographs with a loupe he'd bought, the clarity was amazing and he had no difficulties in identifying the landmarks important to him.

He decided to go to the pub just around the corner, there were a bunch of Irishmen he fell in with and got wrecked. He staggered back to the hotel after midnight, got into bed and sparked out – he hadn't checked his phone.

It was going to be one of those days. With a head pounding he looked at his watch -10am, he felt dreadful which wasn't like him at all – he didn't even know what day it was. Drinking a scalding coffee he gradually came to his senses. He checked his mobile and was horrified to see a message had come through at 6.30pm last night - £2,000, be at tradesmen's entrance 9pm tomorrow – he had to check with Gazelle about the money before answering.

To make matters worse he ran down the stairs, tripped and banged his head, nicked his brow on something and he was bleeding like a stuck pig. He had to return to his room to patch himself up – as he did so he a message came through – Ok to proceed. By now it was 12 noon. He texted the Russian to say OK.

The taxi pulled up outside the embassy, he was bang on time. Ringing the door bell for the third time the door finally opened and a man wearing white dungarees admitted him – he said nothing but held his hand out. At that point Irina appeared and told Gallagher to give the cash to the man and to follow her.

She led him down three flights of dimly lit concrete stairs, it stank of piss. At the bottom was a steel door enclosing an equally dimly lit long narrow room – the shooting range, it was incredibly humid and smelly – all very ancient.

On a table was an embassy owned Dragunov rifle with scope and some 7.62mm ammunition – nothing was said. They both put on ear defenders and flash protector goggles. She clipped a target onto an overhead wire and pulled the pulley system to take it to the far end of the range – 500 metres. Adopting a kneeling position she loaded the rifle with a six round clip and adjusted the scope before firing a single round. Gallagher, looking through a scope could just about see that the round was off target, too far to the right.

She made an adjustment to the knurled wheel on the scope, levelled the rifle and fired five rounds in rapid succession. After removing the empty clip she checked there wasn't a round up the spout and put the rifle back on the table.

They removed the defenders and goggles before she wound the target back to them. There seemed to be only two holes in the target, one to the right of centre and seemingly one in the bull, in fact it was five, virtually in the same hole.

Gallagher was impressed. He left and went to have something to eat, he still felt terrible and his head throbbed. After eating, and not at his allocated time, he sent a text to his link man – Russian good, proceed asap.

Stone and Callan spent a couple of days looking into the Sheikh's personal life, nothing untoward was found, no criminal record but they did discover the enormous fees he charged for his consultancy work – mostly the NHS. They found an address for him, a ground floor apartment in a Victorian villa in a small, leafy street off Haverstock Hill near the Royal Free Hospital.

She decided that the two of them should do a twenty-four hour stake-out of the property to see what, if anything, they could learn. Armed with sleeping bags, flasks and sandwich boxes they set off in a pool car – it was 7am.

They parked about two hundred yards beyond the property using the rear-view mirror to observe, and waited. Nothing happened for over three hours – Stone, who was in the driver's seat, was breaking her neck for a pee. She drove off to a garage on the main road, as she got to the T junction at the end of the road she saw in the mirror the suspect leaving his home. She told Callan to get out and follow, she would catch up with him.

He was about five hundred yards behind the suspect who turned right at the main road Gazelle, highly trained, instinctively knew he was being followed. He carried on for a few hundred yards then turned suddenly retracing his steps, he carried on past Callan who was wearing a yellow windcheater then suddenly he turned again. As Gazelle passed

Callan, now going in the opposite direction, he knew for certain who his tail was, – an old but effective ploy.

Callan could do nothing. His mobile rang, it was Stone asking where he was, he told her that he'd been rumbled and gave his location. She went there and cruised down the road looking for the suspect; amazingly she spotted him just going into a coffee shop. She stopped and watched. He sat by a window alone. She called Callan and told him to join her.

He got into the car and started taking photographs but, because they were at an oblique angle, he knew there would be reflections – they couldn't move any closer without being seen – she told him to take off his yellow jacket. Approaching them on the opposite side of the road was a tall attractive blond, she went into the coffee shop and after looking around joined the suspect – she needed to know who this woman was.

Callan asked what she was doing as she drove off. Half a mile down the road she turned the car around and drove back double parking almost opposite the shop and causing an obstruction, she was taking a chance but she needed a photograph. Callan managed to get a few good shots before irate drivers started blowing horns, they drove off.

"Right I want you to go back to the office and start on the images, try and find out who she is. I'm going to hang around here and follow her when she comes out of the shop."

It was just starting to rain and she didn't have a coat or umbrella, she went and stood in a shop doorway waiting, it was pouring down. Forty minutes later, the rain still tipping down, a cab pulled up in front of the coffee shop, the blonde rushed out straight into it.

Sod it! She said to herself. There was no way she would be able to hail another cab and follow, she'd had bitter experiences when trying to get a cab in London when it was raining; so she had to make do with taking the licence number and calling it through to Callan asking him to call the dispatcher to see where the Russian was taken.

When the rain eased off she did get a cab to home where she could change into dry clothes before going to Thames House.

"She got out at Tottenham Hale," said Callan as she arrived at her desk.

"Have you found out anything about her?"

"Nothing yet, I'm running the image through image recognition but it's a slow job."

"Okay. Let the Met have an image and ask them to keep their eyes open in the Tottenham area. Attractive blond, about 6 feet tall, around twelve stone, possibly Scandinavian or Russian, do not apprehend, just watch her and report back."

Her mobile rang - it was Matt to see when she could make dinner. She apologised and explained she was up to her eyes in it at the moment and she would call him. She thought afterwards she'd sounded brusque – poor chap, she didn't mean it.

Gazelle was rather taken with the Russian, extremely attractive he thought but, dangerous eyes. She wanted more detail before discussing her fee.

"When will I know who I'm supposed to shoot, where and when?"

"It is not important for you to know who the target is - Seamus Gallagher will be with you. The location is in East Anglia, an area north east of London. We are waiting to fix a time and date and I will let you know."

Eventually they agreed on a fee of £120,000 - £80,000 payable in advance; the remaining £40,000 to be paid on completion – all in cash.

Looking out of the window they could see some idiot had double parked opposite and there was one hell of a noise as people were sounding their horns. They also agreed that Gallagher would contact her once they had a date and then pay her the advance payment.

It was now a question of waiting, waiting for the vital intelligence on the Duke's schedule.

Gallagher had a problem. He didn't have driving licence with the same name as any of his debit cards, He hadn't needed to use a card as cash had been accepted when necessary, but he didn't think that would work with an airline. He thought for a moment before ringing a contact in London who he knew could arrange a fake licence in the name on his debit card; he also needed a DVLA code, he would use his 'safe house' as the address. He made a phone call and twenty four hours later he met up with a man in a pub at St Pancras – he walked out with what he needed £200 the lighter. This time he was Michael Collins.

Using the internet connection of his phone for the first time he booked a one way flight from London City to Inverness and arranged to hire a car from outside Inverness airport, just in case those hire firms at the airport were on the alert – he wasn't taking any chances.

From Inverness he drove cautiously to Fort William, then Ballachulish and took the coastal road to Oban – he never saw a police car all the way home.

Chapter
18

Gazelle was taking stock. He was pleased – everything was falling into place. Hammond and his link man were on a five day training course on Hovercrafts in Southampton, they had two days to go. The sniper had been organised and the rifle should arrive this week - that had cost £8,000.

There were two items outstanding; Gallagher's final plan and the crucial intelligence on the Duke of Cambridge's movements from his contact at Kensington Palace.

Gallagher stopped off to get some provisions in Oban, fish in particular – what better place to get it. He turned his mobile on to see if there were any messages before he went out of range, there were none. He had got permission from Gazelle to use the phone more frequently; this was okay provided he turned it off when not using it.

From bright sunshine the sky filled with ominous clouds. It started to rain like it only does on the west coast of Scotland – stair rods. He got to the remote cottage to a warm welcome from Trevor.

Next morning Gallagher started to finalise his plans. There were a number of elements that had to work in his favour that he no control over. Assuming that the target was going to be in place he was gambling that he would be at the swimming pool in the grounds of the hall, just to the left of the mansion; the weather would need to be good. He knew the Duke was a keen swimmer and the large pool had only just been constructed.

When he had a date he would check the tide tables for the Norfolk coast. He established the timings of the gamekeeper's rounds when they were criss-crossing the Estate and it was clear the attempt would have to be made between 11am and 2pm – just a three hour gap.

He spent some time poring over the OS map and aerial photographs checking the position the sniper would have to be in, and their escape route.

Concerned about how to keep the rifle out of sight, it was 50 inches long – he needed to think. A coffee was required. He went the kitchen to heat up the kettle on the wood burning range, Trevor wasn't there, he was probably out painting – it was a nice morning. He took his coffee outside but that didn't last long, it was very humid and the midges started biting immediately so he retreated indoors – it reminded him of the mosquitoes around the marshes of Basra

He was assuming Gazelle was organising the Hovercraft, cross country motorbike and getaway car but he must check. Thinking about logistics a venue should be chosen with a provisional time for a briefing of all involved – probably London – this must all be conveyed to Gazelle sooner rather than later.

Tripods - would a carrying case for one be suitable to hold the rifle thus disguising it he asked himself. He would go to Oban tomorrow, he had seen two photographic shops there; he could go and measure some to see.

This meeting was in the SIS building at Vauxhall, the usual were present – it was 7.30am.

"Operation Jonah - over to you Nat."

"Not much progress at the moment sir. Our man, the Sheikh, had a meeting with a woman in Hampstead and we are still trying to identify her. I haven't found anything detrimental on the Sheikh yet but we're still looking……." Her mobile rang, she excused herself and left the room to take the call – it was Callan.

"This blonde woman, Irina Kowlowski, is known to our friends over the pond. Just over two years ago the CIA had her under surveillance in Aleppo. She's thought to be a freelance special ops working for the Russians. She served in the Russian army as a major from 1999 to 2014 when she went solo - present whereabouts unknown."

There was silence for a moment.

"Do we know what her speciality was?"

"Hang on," he was tapping his keyboard - "Sniper."

"Okay, thanks Callan."

She went back into the room, McLeod was talking.

"We've just had this come through from our guys in Cairo," she spread half a dozen photos on the table. This guy was killed in a gun battle with the police in Cairo just a few hours ago along with three others; they were believed to be terrorists and members of the Muslim Brotherhood.

"They know three of them but not this one," she said pointing to the dead man. She slid another image across the table for all to see.

"This same guy was photographed by us in Cairo taking to our friend the Sheikh."

There was a pause.

"Excuse me sir but I've got some important information here."

"Carry on Nat."

She reported what Callan had told her.

"This is beginning to make sense," said Simmonds. We've now got a Russian sniper, the Muslim Brotherhood, a squeaky clean Egyptian surgeon, Hammond and Gallagher/Gilligan, the latter knows the surgeon. Let's go around the table with this."

"Ned."

"We've not had any further suspicious activity at Balmoral or Sandringham but we have stepped up our security so a lack of activity shouldn't be surprise. The Duke of Cambridge will be at Anmer Hall in fifteen days' time and we will be doubling our presence for that visit."

"How many will that contingency account for?"

"Forty-two officers while he's there. But, he really doesn't like any intrusion by us so we have to keep our heads down – he's just like his grandfather, Prince Phillip.

"We had a couple of arrests this week for threatening behaviour, one at Windsor and the other at Hampton Court but nothing else suspicious.

"Now we have the names of these individuals why don't we nip any plot in the bud and pull them in, as we agreed with overall policy?"

"Okay, let's hear what Betine has to say."

"I still think we should wait. I know we agreed to go in earlier but this seems to be an entirely new cell. We should continue gathering information to see where it leads us, I get the feeling whoever is heading this is a very big fish. We know the location of Hammond and the Sheikh but we don't know where the Russian is or Gallagher/Gilligan so we couldn't around them all up any way."

"Good point," said Boswell. "I agree; we should direct our efforts to finding these two."

"We're agreed then; we'll step up our efforts to find them. Nat, please give us an update regarding this."

"Yes sir. The Met are going from business to business in the Tottenham area, I think that's where she lives. Fortunately, we have a good image of her and, if I'm right, we should find her soon.

"As for Gallagher/Gilligan, I've asked Police Scotland to step up their search for him. They're focussing on the Oban area because he was vaguely coming from that direction when stopped. They are going from business to business with an image as in Tottenham - it's a long shot but it's the best we've got at the moment.

"I think we should increase surveillance on the Sheikh and start watching Hammond again, I know it's expensive with all the resources required but sooner or later, if we're right, all of them have to come together at some point."

Simmonds, looking around the table said, "What do you think of Nat's suggestion?" The other two nodded their agreement.

Stone got lucky less than twenty-four hours later. An off-duty police sergeant was shopping with his wife in Oban, he almost ran into Gallagher as he was going into Mackie's rod and gun shop in the High Street – Gallagher was coming out.

It took a moment or two for Gallagher's visage to register in the sergeant's mind – the walls of the police station were plastered with it. He went straight back out - his wife was looking in the window. "Did you see that man come out?"

"Yes, he went down there," she said pointing toward the harbour.

He walked off at a pace calling the police station on his mobile as he went, he couldn't see the suspect, where had he gone he asked himself. The word went out to all patrolling officers immediately with the caveat, do not apprehend.

Another officer on traffic control at road-works spotted the suspect coming out of Oban Music, a shop near the harbour. He radioed the sighting through and this was relayed to the sergeant who picked him up and started following him, he went into another music shop and then Oban Photographic – the sergeant hung around. He waited for nearly forty minutes until the suspect came out carrying two long black plastic tubes about 12 inches in diameter and 50 to 60 inches long – a bit like a piece of drainpipe.

Giving a running commentary on his mobile he followed the suspect to the main car park in the town. Someone else was sent to the shops visited to see what the suspect wanted while the sergeant watched him get into his car – he reported the registration number. A CID officer came on the line asking if he could follow – he couldn't, his car was parked in a different part of the town.

A patrol car was instructed to follow the suspect at a discreet distance, radioing his location as he went. Police Scotland's own helicopter for

Argyll was out of service but they regularly cooperated with the Scottish Air Ambulance and called them up on the radio.

By good fortune, their helicopter was airborne with an injured climber en route to Glasgow from Mull – the pilot was asked to pick up the patrol car on the Oban to Lochgilphead Road, its number on the roof was 072. They found it without difficulty but the weather was closing in so they couldn't delay for long.

The following police officer was instructed to stop the pursuit. The bright yellow Air Ambulance helicopter, a familiar sight in the Argyll skies, took over. A police helicopter scrambled at Glasgow was flying towards Oban; once they knew the route the suspect was taking they would take over.

About ten miles outside Oban the suspect turned left, heading for Glen Lonan, an isolated route to Taynuilt. The police helicopter flew over the suspect going in the opposite direction and then kept well away hovering at about 3,000 feet, the co-pilot was watching through powerful binoculars. Cleverly the pilot had positioned the helicopter with the sun, which was reappearing, directly behind them therefore even had the suspect been looking he couldn't see them - the Air Ambulance helicopter continued to Glasgow.

The suspect's car wound its way through the Glen, at about the halfway point it turned to the right, up a track to a white painted cottage set by trees and a burn which, even at that distant, could be seen to be a white, raging torrent after a recent downpour. The GPS coordinates were radioed through to the police in Oban.

The CID officer poring over the large scale map of the area soon spotted that the location of the cottage in Glen Lonan would be impossible to monitor - there was nowhere to watch it from without being spotted – he was dreading the cost implications and what it would do for the station's budget if they were given instructions to carry out surveillance.

Gallagher had been looking for some sort of container in the shops he'd visited. Success came when he purchased two tubes for a camera tripod and a tripod at Oban Photographic.

Back in London Simmonds was being given a blow-by-blow account of what was happening over the telephone, Stone was in the room with him. He guessed what the tube was for – to conceal the sniper's rifle, but why two tubes.

"Three down, one to go," he said. "We just need to find this Russian before our next move."

Chapter

19

Still no sign of the Russian, although at one shop on Seven Sister's Road the assistant thought she recognised the suspect, apparently she went to the shop occasionally – the police staked out the premises. A look-a-like did turn up late in the afternoon but it wasn't who they were looking for – the search continued.

Anmer 20 to 23/6. That was the message received by Gazelle from his contact at Kensington Palace, today was the 7th June – thirteen days. He'd thought long and hard about this moment, the venue to get the whole team together – all his recruits and the Russian for a briefing. An airborne conference was the solution.

Gazelle needed a quiet airport and decided on Humberside, not far from the Humber bridge and mostly used by charter flights. He booked a private charter, a Dassault Falcon jet seating fourteen passengers at noon for three days hence. He made sure that it had swivel seats and provision for a white board; he declined the use of a steward and said he wanted a round trip, without landing, to the Bay of Biscay - well within the jet's range. Text messages were sent to all involved.

Simmonds, with Stone as his second in command, allocated a team of four people to each suspect – two on two off. These were a mixture of police, MI5 and a couple of special protection officers, there were others in reserve and further support from Police Scotland. Hammond's car had a tracker; the Sheikh didn't appear to have a car and none appeared to be registered in his name.

Because of Gallagher's location an unmarked police car was stationed at each end of Glen Lonan, it was the best they could do, but there were no roads off the Glen, apart from at each end.

Thirteen days to go.

Gallagher wouldn't know of any of the arrangements until he was in range of a mobile signal. He'd completed his plan and was pleased with it. When he'd finished packing his car, not forgetting his camouflage jacket, he was off to Inverness airport to fly back to London. He told Trevor not to forget to put the dustbin at the end of the drive – he would tow it down on the back of his old Citroen 2CV.

The cottage was owned by Gallagher but in the name of Gilligan, annually he would go into Oban to pay his council tax in cash – they had no other services apart from the dustbin collection once a fortnight.

He was wondering where he was going to put the two bulky tripod tubes until he needed them when his mobile bleeped, he stopped to read the text message, he'd just come into range. At last he thought to himself. He didn't notice the blue Mondeo parked in a lay-by as he turned right onto the Oban road. He was going back the way he had come, by Ballachulish – it started to rain heavily. Before he went any further he drove to the harbour to find a chandlers – he needed a copy of the UK tide tables.

Once the two cars had cleared the Connel Bridge just outside Oban the police officer radioed ahead to Fort William for the police there to take over – they did when Gallagher arrived and followed him to the airport without incident. Police were waiting when he got back to London. Now they'd got him they weren't going to let him go at any cost. He took a cab with his two bulky tubes to a B&B in Islington, they followed at a distance.

When Simmonds learnt of the tide tables he was puzzled, Stone too.

Twelve days to go

The hairdresser in Northumberland Park did recognise the tall blonde. She told the WPC that she didn't know where the woman lived, but she did have a mobile number in case of cancellations – the woman had been in two days earlier, she wasn't a regular. It was a Russian mobile provider, they had to try something else; the number alone wouldn't help at all.

Stone joined in, she had an idea. Not far from Tottenham going into London there's a Russian club, she passed it often on the bus. She went to visit armed with a photograph of the woman. It was dark inside and stank of tobacco regardless of the smoking ban; there weren't many customers – it was a seedy place. Yes, she was a regular customer and a member said the receptionist, no they couldn't divulge her address because of confidentiality. Stone asked to see the manager and explained to him who she was, she had to show her ID.

"Why do you need this information?" he said in a thick accent.

"All I can tell you is it's for National Security reasons."

As a Russian he was aware of the implications if he didn't comply with such a request in his own country, he gave her the address in Anthill Road, Tottenham.

Yes! A result!

Surveillance was set up immediately.

Four out of four she said to herself. She went back to the office and reported to Simmonds.

What she didn't know was that the woman she was looking for was in the club too, she'd just collected a rifle in a black, soft gun slip from Tilbury docks and was hiding it in the club; she overheard the conversation with the manager.

The Russian immediately caught a cab to her lodgings in Tottenham, grabbed her bags and left in the cab that had waited for her – she got out just in time.

Eleven days to go

Gazelle was at his home going through his checklist, he was fully conscious of the unmarked police car sitting down the road - pressure was building. He knew that the police knew of him, Gallagher and Hammond, he wasn't sure about the Russian woman – they would probably make a move soon he was thinking. But, he argued with himself, what would they be charged with – they hadn't done anything wrong. The only charge he could think of would be conspiracy to perform a terrorist act but, with a decent lawyer, he was certain that wouldn't stick.

The rifle was awaiting collection at Tilbury docks, the Russian was going to pick it up – she'd been paid her advance of £80,000 so that was now her responsibility.

A second-hand three man Hovercraft and trailer had been bought and along with a stolen scrambler bike, a stolen Subaru Legacy and a stolen Ford Fiesta was in a rented barn in Norfolk – he was confident the police were unaware of these four pieces of equipment or their whereabouts and there would be no paper trail leading to him. The Subaru was being re-painted, white instead of green and false number plates were being fixed to that, the motorbike and the Ford. He was beginning to use the other members of the team now.

Hammond and his link man had both passed their Hovercraft training with flying colours – they were proficient.

Chapter
20

Ten days to go

Humberside airport is not the easiest place to get to, but everyone arrived and they were gathered in a private lounge. Some had come by car, some by train and taxi and two by plane, the only one they were waiting for was the Russian.

Gazelle looked at his watch 10.15am – still plenty of time – he wasn't worried; he knew she wouldn't dare renege on their deal. He'd checked in with the Cook's Charter Travel (CCT) without baggage, he'd instructed the others to do the same – all had their passports.

This was a fraught period as he knew that at least three of them will have been followed to the airport by police. It was entirely possible that when the Russian arrived they'd move in and arrest them all.

Simmonds, McLeod, Boswell and Stone were listening in to reports from the police on a secure conference line in London. They had established that the pilot of the charter flight the group was taking had submitted a flight plan to fly to the Bay of Biscay and back without landing, it will take 5 hour and forty minutes according to the plan."

"The 64,000 dollar question is, do we grab them all as soon as the Russian appears, wait until they get back or leave them be for the time being?"

"When the Russian arrives there will be ten of them – who are the ones we don't know?" asked McLeod

"We haven't established that yet, but if we let them take off they'll have to go through passport control and security, then we'll have all their details and plenty of time to find that out," replied Simmonds.

He continued. "We still don't know for certain whom the target is and where their operation will be. My guess is it's the Duke of Cambridge and probably Anmer, but it is a guess. I also guess the getaway will involve a boat because we know Gallagher bought a copy of the UK tide tables.

"Have you heard anything at all Betine? It seems strange that we haven't had a whisper from somewhere."

"Not a dicky-bird Max, I agree, it is strange. It's even gone quiet on the infrastructure plot – weird I must admit."

"Anything at your end Ned?"

"No, but we have been putting motion sensors in the woods around Anmer Hall, they are driving everyone nuts with false alarms so we might have to remove them. It's interesting that you mention a boat, Anmer is not far from the sea - I'll send some men to the coast to ask around. We've been carrying out manoeuvres around Anmer so I think we are well prepared for any attack."

"May I sir?" asked Stone with her hand raised as if in school - everyone chuckled at the sight.

"Of course," said her boss.

"I am presuming they are all meeting for some sort of briefing. They know they're taking a risk and will know that some of them are being tailed by us, but it seems essential they're all together. We don't seem to have anything other than a conspiracy charge against them and I don't think we'll gain anything by pulling them now, if we're going to do it at all then we have to have intelligence beforehand."

"And how do you propose we get that intelligence Nat?"

There was silence for a moment.

She responded. "I think the key may be with one of these other men we know nothing about yet. Once we have their details we can see if we can find weak spots with any of them, and then persuade them to give us the required intelligence."

Another silence.

McLeod was the first to speak. "I think Nat is right, we've got to have inside access if we're going to crack this."

"So are we saying let them carry on for the time being?" asked Simmonds.

Everyone nodded in acquiescence.

"I've been trying to look into this Gallagher/Gilligan character that I met in Iraq and I have had the same problem as you Nat – I can't get anywhere. What I want to know is why he was there – who invited him and in what capacity?"

"Hang on a minute Betine, I just need to tell police to let them go," Simmonds called them.

"Sorry, please carry on."

"Unfortunately our ambassador is now dead and the first secretary was killed in the fire bomb attack, none of those surviving knows anything about him. In his file we're told he was an undercover cop in Ireland – do you have anything on this Max?"

"I've not come up with anything to substantiate that, but it would have been in my predecessor's time, like the ambassador Sir John is now dead so I can't ask him. I see where you're going with this Betine and I guess it's possible he is an undercover agent, but surely that would be your department – wouldn't it?"

"Well it's not." She could be short sometimes, her manner,

Once the Russian arrived the gleaming Dassault Falcon jet in grey and white livery took off on schedule. The information and images of all on board would shortly be arriving at Thames House electronically.

Chapter
21

When the aircraft got to cruising altitude the seats were swivelled round to face aft, the white board provided by the airline was assembled and an annotated copy of the area of the OS map they were interested in, and a pen and pad was handed to everyone.

Gazelle took the floor.

"Thank you all for being here for this momentous meeting. Soon we shall be able to complete our glorious mission to destroy the infidel's love and belief in their Royal family."

The Russian hadn't heard any of this before; she didn't know what to make of it. After consideration she decided it wasn't her problem – she was being paid a substantial amount of cash to do a job.

"This operation is going to require a lot of discipline to be a success, if any of you have any doubts then you must say so now."

Silence.

"Okay. I am going to hand over to G (Gallagher) to explain the wonderful operational plan that he has drawn up."

Gallagher stood up and went to the white board. He drew a rough plan of Anmer Hall, the four roads that surround it and the belts of woodland. He explained this to his audience – it was like a military briefing, well in many ways it was and it was evident the he'd done this before.

"No questions until I have finished. We know our target will be at this location from the 20th to 23rd June but we do not have a time. It is presumed the weather will be fine and the target will use their newly constructed swimming pool and that's where they will be hit.

"Each of you is expected to arrive in the area individually two days before our target appears and to find somewhere to stay, some of you might want to camp, some might want to hire a camper van – these are common sights around the area. You are all holidaymakers and some of you are birdwatchers too. Two of you at least should carry binoculars and cameras – decide who amongst yourselves.

"The area is heavily policed therefore diversions will be needed to enable us, me and our sniper, to get into position," he pointed to the edge of some woodland overlooking the Hall. "We will remain there between the hours of 11.00 and 14.00; we will repeat this on the second and third day if necessary.

"From early on the first morning H (Hammond) and A (his link man) will collect the Hovercraft from the storage barn marked on your map and take it to Brancaster on the coast, it too is marked on your map, you should accommodate yourselves there as well. You will use the craft as if you are on holiday – get people used to seeing it.

"If the tide is right our sniper's escape route will be to take a prearranged launch from the small harbour there, very high tides are listed for both days. If the tide is wrong then the Hovercraft will take the sniper across the marshes to the launch that will be waiting offshore – marked on your map. That launch will then deliver her to Wells harbour that has a deep water channel and a taxi can be hired there. Hovercrafts are not that unusual in the area as the lifeboat services (RNLI) use them. You will repeat these instructions until we arrive at Brancaster – if, after three days we haven't appeared then disperse.

"Two of you, B and D, will go to the storage barn to collect a blue Ford Fiesta, the barn is marked on your map. No later than 10.30 you should park it on this hard standing, here on your map," he said pointing to the location. "Leave the key on top of the off-side rear wheel; there will be a dog bed on the seat suggesting the car belongs to a dog walker. D, you will collect a motorbike and bring it to here, by the woodland marked on your map, after picking up B - no later than 10.45; it's all off-road. Both of you should wear a camouflage jacket and forage cap.

"The rest of you will need to arrive in dribs and drabs between 10.00 and 10.30. If you have a camouflage jacket wear it - don't forget your cameras and binoculars. You assemble by this woodland marked on your map," gesturing to the white board again.

"Don't completely block the road with your vehicles but park messily so as to impede any traffic. You will be called Twitchers – bird watchers to anyone who asks and you have had word on the grapevine of a sea eagle in the area. You must appear to be unknown to each other. Let's take a break and then we'll have questions, refreshments are in the overhead lockers."

After twenty minutes or so the meeting resumed. The Russian had the first questions.

"Are there likely to be any dog patrols?"

"I've not seen any but, as a precaution, I will have a pepper based Capsaicin spray with me that we can use as a deodorant."

"What about movement sensors in the woodland?"

"I think it unlikely because of the abundant wildlife moving around, but I don't know for sure – it's a risk."

"Is the target likely to be in the light or shade – indoors or outdoors?"

All very professional questions.

"We are hoping they will be in or around the swimming pool."

"I shall be carrying the rifle in a black soft gun slip what shall I do with the gun once I've shot the target?"
"Leave it there. I'm assuming you will be wearing gloves so there will not be any fingerprints."

"Yes very fine Latex. How do I get away from the location to the coast?"

"You will come with me on the motorbike, then by car."

"Okay, thank you."

"What if the police ask what we are doing?" asked B.

"Tell them you are bird watching, if they want your details then give them; they have no record of you. The same applies to everyone except G and H."

Another of the group asked what they were to do if the target didn't turn up.

"If our intelligence is good then they will, if not then disperse after the third day.

The point of the bird watching is a diversion, there is a hotline to let Twitchers know of a sighting and I will use to tell of the sea eagle, plenty of people will arrive giving us adequate cover – it should be pretty chaotic. If need be I'm certain we can create the same situation twice or even three times. Remember your own experiences of someone pointing to the sky – everyone around will look as well – we can use that trick.

"Any more questions?"

The Russian spoke again.

"When will I receive the balance of my fee?"

"At Brancaster harbour," said Gallagher.

There followed a silence.

"Okay, you all know what to do, make sure your telephones are fully charged although reception in that area is not good – texts only, no calls. Irina, you will meet me at Kings Lynn station at 08.30 on the first morning – that's the 06.45 train from King's Cross, London. If anyone asks you about the gun slip say you are going to a clay pigeon shoot."

Gazelle stood up. "Excellent G, very clear and concise. It's difficult to see where it can go wrong. Good luck to you all and May Allah Be with You."

Stone and Callan, back at HQ were going through the names and images of those on the charter flight. She zeroed in on one in particular, Mustapha Badru – it rang a loud bell. Aged 32 born in Baghdad. She called the surname up, there was no Mustapha but, there was Alim Badru, she'd sat in on his questioning with Tyson at the Yard – were they connected - brothers or cousins perhaps? She compared photographs – yes, there was a likeness.

"What time do they get back to Humberside Nat?"

She looked at her watch. "Just under an hour."

"Right, follow him and once we have more intel we'll pull him in for questioning. Do not pull him at the airport – is that clear?"

"Yes sir. What do we tell him as to why he's being questioned?"

"At this stage tell him we would like him to assist us with our enquiries, a matter of national importance. If he resists then up the ante and tell him they are terrorist related enquiries – whatever, don't let him have access to communications."

"Should we pull him, or the Met?"

"Hmm – the Met, I'll have a word with Commander Tyson. I want you to do the interview, I will be watching; there will be a red light opposite where you'll be sitting, if it comes on then stop. Remember we are not arresting or charging this man so keep it relaxed and informal. If I think I'm needed, then I will join you."

After the jet had landed everyone disembarked, there were no delays at immigration; they were the only customers. They dispersed at two minute intervals, Hammond, Gallagher, the Sheikh, the Russian and now Badru were followed; the latter led his followers to his home in Pilkington Street, West London – surveillance was set up shortly after.

Chapter

22

Nine days to go

Hoping she wasn't being over confident she'd anticipated she would be given this job. She had a strategy; the technique taught by her boss – wherever possible know the answers to the questions you are going to put, that way you'll soon know if the suspect is lying. She and Callan furiously set about discovering everything there was to know about Mustapha Badru.

Born Baghdad 1984, one brother, one sister (names not known), father a banker. Mustapha and his father fled to Britain twelve years ago and were given political asylum. Another sister and his mother had been killed in an air raid. He gained a scholarship to Haberdashers school and went on to Radley where he excelled. Married with a four year old child, his wife is a lawyer. He set up a financial services business three years ago – it was flourishing, he had two partners both, British. He seemed squeaky clean, no criminal record and not even an endorsement on his licence.

Mustapha Badru was dreading the day the knock on the door would come. He had no intension of being subversive to the country that had taken in him and his family –he'd been brainwashed, radicalised, the trip to the Madrassa had the desired effect.

He had little choice but to accept the policeman's request to come to the police station – just a couple of hours he said, nothing to worry about sir, we just want to ask you some questions. No there's no need for a solicitor, it's just a chat and then we will bring you back.

The function room at the Yard was light and airy, an attractive young woman and a uniformed sergeant were seated at the large table in comfortable chairs; a jug of coffee sat on the table. Badru was shown in.

"Good morning Mr Badru," said Stone. "Please take a seat – would you like a coffee?"

"Yes please."

"This is an informal chat, the meeting is not being recorded and no charges are being brought, we just need to ask you a few questions. Could you please confirm that your name is Mustapha Badru?"

"Yes."

"Please tell me your place and date of birth."

"Baghdad, the 15th January 1984."

"Thank you. What is your employment?"

"I am a director of a financial services company."

She poured a coffee while talking.

"Sugar, milk?" she asked.

"No thank you."

She paused while pouring herself a coffee.

"Is your business doing well?"

"All is good at the moment."

"I understand that you live in a nice house in west London, married to a beautiful wife and you have a lovely daughter, it must be very different for you from when you were in Baghdad."

"It is, I am very lucky."

"Have you been abroad lately Mr Badru?"

He hesitated for a moment.

"Yes, well sort of."

"What do you mean by sort of?"

"Yesterday I went on a flight to the Bay of Biscay and back, we did not land anywhere. It was a business trip, a seminar about security in the financial sector."

"Is that a normal way to have a meeting?"

"No, it was unusual."

She took a photograph of Alim Badru from the folder on the table and slid it across.

"Do you know this man Mr Badru?"

He said no far too quickly and slid the image back.

"Are you certain? Have another look."

"No Why should I? Who is he?"

"His name is Alim Badru."

"It's a common name in my country."

"He is suspected of being involved with terrorist activities."

Mustapha looked decidedly nervous.

"She took another image from the folder – The Sheikh - and slid it over.

"Do you recognise this man?"

He said nothing. This was the critical moment.

"I think I need a lawyer before I answer any more of your questions. I would like to go now please." He stood up.

"You have no need of a lawyer Mr Badru, we are not arresting you or charging you with anything. Just a few more questions if you don't mind."

Simmonds, on the edge of his seat, in the adjacent room was listening in and watching Badru's reactions on CCTV.

"I'm going to level with you Mr Badru. We are concerned about the people on yesterday's flight and your involvement with them. Some, but not all of the other passengers are known to us. Now can I ask you again if you recognise this man?" She slid the image of the Sheikh over again.

"I want to go."

Her voice firmed, she now sounded menacing. "Running away isn't going to solve this problem Mr Badru. Do you want your wife and business partners to know about this meeting?"

She sensed his character was weak and naïve.

"That's blackmail!"

"No. I would call it an opportunity to cooperate with us."

He was visibly shaken and she didn't let up.

"Why don't you tell me what exactly that flight was about?"

Elbows resting on the table he buried his head in his hands. He was in a corner and he knew it.

Simmonds was pleased, incredible ability he said to himself, she'll go far.

"Okay Mr Badru, that's enough, we'll take you home now. Have a think about our chat and call me, here's my number. Thank you for your help and cooperation."

He was driven home in silence. Seeing his world was collapsing around him he was in a panic. If he told the police Gazelle would have him killed, or worse, his family too, he knew the dark side of the Brotherhood. If he told Gazelle then the police would ruin his life and he would end up in prison.

After getting home to a worried wife he placated her by explaining that it was a case of mistaken identity – another man with the same surname – nothing to do with him, everything was alright.

He decided on the lesser of two evils and called Gazelle on his mobile. He thought it almost certain there was a tap on his landline.

"I am sorry to report sir that I was questioned by the police today. They thought I was related to Alim Badru, my cousin, but I said I wasn't and they let that go. They knew all about our flight yesterday and who was on board. I think they know a lot more and they are trying to blackmail me into helping them. What should I do?"

"Let me think, I will call you back, probably tomorrow, but don't worry."

Chapter
23

Eight days to go

He was worried and didn't sleep that night because he was beginning to think he should tell the police. He went to his car just after seven the next morning, as he approached it another car pulled up, the driver's window opened and three shots were fired, Mustapha fell to the floor with a spreading pool of blood around him, he was dead less than a minute later.

"Bugger! I thought I had him," said Stone to her boss when she received the news.

"You can't win them all Nat. It was a good idea as we have no hard evidence of a plot, an insider would have helped. Do you think it's worth trying the same idea with one of the others?"

"Assuming the Sheikh, or one of that group killed Mustapha they will all have been warned so, no, there would be no takers in my view."

Gazelle was known as a hard man, he had no qualms in having Mustapha Badru killed, there must be no weak links in the chain; this was a warning to the others. Nothing will interfere with his project - he still had the advantage in this game of chess with the authorities.

Sadly, a number of the suspects that were being tailed from the airport were lost; the Lincolnshire constabulary just wasn't up to the task. Irina Kowlowski rang rings around her two followers and disappeared in London, they were bewildered by the London underground, she hadn't mastered it either but she was a darn sight better than the two coppers.

She got someone from the club where she was hiding to drive her, under cover of darkness, to the Russian embassy and wait; she didn't want to be seen carrying the rifle in its slip around London. The scope of the rifle needed zeroing after its travels, it may have received a knock that would've affected its accuracy and she needed to be fully prepared for the task ahead. She got into the prone position and fired several shots, making adjustments to the scope in between, before she was satisfied. Then, using fuse wire, she carefully wired the knurled adjuster of the scope into place; it couldn't move thus ensuring it would remain zeroed.

Seven days to go

Gazelle's last instructions to his team had been to keep their heads down for a few days, let the authorities keep guessing. He told them to get their transport and accommodation organised and to make sure any equipment they were going to use was fully prepared.

"The real danger here is this Russian sniper, we've got to find her," said Simmonds. Only two of the heads were present at the meeting, McLeod had called to say she'd been delayed.

"Could you give us an update on her please Nat."

"I have been wondering how she knew we had her address in Tottenham, she got out of there just in time so she must have been warned. The only person who had that address was me and the manager of the Russian club. Either he warned her, or she, or someone else, was there and overheard the conversation. The manager was terrified of me so my guess is she was there and maybe still is."

McLeod, out of breath joined the meeting. "I'm so sorry but we have a high alert on. We've had reliable word through GCHQ that an attack on three of London's main reservoirs with poison is imminent. We had a whisper about this a while ago but nothing since. We have to assume it's yet another new terrorist cell or, it's related to operation Jonah."

"Just what we didn't need," said Simmonds. "Why do you think it might be connected to Jonah?"

"Do you remember the man with the fez that our man in Cairo followed? He turned up dead after a shoot-out with the police; he was known as Mansour. They took a while to find where he lived but, when they did they turned up some interesting material.

"Firstly there was some correspondence, some of it was with someone called Gazelle; word has it that he is a senior member of the Muslim Brotherhood. It referred to an attack on infrastructure and the Royal family in the UK. There were also some sketches of a reservoir in Walthamstow with the Ferry Boat inn written in pencil to one side. In the café in Cairo Mansour was photographed with our Sheikh– are he and this Gazelle one and the same?"

"If we assume they are Betine, what does that tell us?"

There was silence for a moment.

Before McLeod could answer Simmonds said, "Nat, you'd better get someone down to that Russian club to keep and eye on it."

She got up and left to give instructions to Callan.

"Betine, you weren't here but Nat had a thought that the Russian might be hiding in the club."

"Back to the question you asked Betine Max, I think we are in the process of being set up. What if this infrastructure plot is a diversion? If it's not it's certainly going to stretch us and our resources including those to safeguard the Royal family," said Ned Boswell.

"You're right Ned; we don't have sufficient resources to handle two major operations like this at the same time. I'm going to have to speak to the Prime Minister. With everything else that's going on he'll have no option other than using the army to protect the reservoirs."

Six days to go

It was a diversion. Gazelle had set it up with Mansour when he was in Cairo.

The plan was that when Mansour received notification then the police were to be informed that he, Mansour, was planning an attack – it never got that far. When the police raided the dead man's livings they found the correspondence including one postcard in the mail box, it simply said 'Go', it was signed Gazelle. The sketches had also been planted - a sophisticated double bluff, just unfortunate that Mansour was killed, that was how Gazelle saw it. The alarm went up in London anyway, so it worked.

Gallagher, back in Argyll now was pondering how to best use the spare tripod tube he'd bought. Trevor had picked him up at Inverness and they had a bumpy ride home in the 2CV, how it ever passed its MOT amazed him – he never felt safe in it.

He'd purchased two of the tripod tubes to confuse his watchers, but he'd succeeded in confusing himself, he was fed up with lugging them around so if he couldn't think of something he would leave the spare one at the cottage.

The large trunk in his room contained numerous oddities, amongst them was some camouflage clothing and, most importantly, his 9mm Colt pistol with its serial number ground off. He set about cleaning it and making sure it functioned properly. Frustrated at having to hang around he and Trevor went walking in the hills for a couple of days, they had a tent and the weather looked good for the moment.

Booking in to a B&B at a pub in the village of Harpley, was the easy bit. Not far from Anmer but he needed to work out how to get there without being followed.

Hammond was busy with his photography but, he too was frustrated at the wait. He guessed his watchers were as well. Apart from visiting clients he drove around on a few occasions just to wind them up.

Stone woke with a start, cold and disorientated. She looked at her watch 02.45. It was her time of the month and, combined with exhaustion, she had fallen asleep in the car. It was parked diagonally opposite the entrance to the Russian club about 200 yards away with a clear view of the entrance, there wasn't a soul about; she'd been asleep for nearly four hours.

Having taken over from Callan who had been watching the place without result it was her turn because they were so short of staff. She hadn't seen the Russian come out of the club or return two hours later while she was sleeping. He was to take over again at 05.00. She poured a black coffee from her flask, ate a sandwich and started to feel a little better.

Admittedly she'd been involved with only a few cases since joining MI5 but they hadn't shown anything like this level of sophistication in their planning.

She was thinking about the Sheikh. Clearly educated and by all accounts a brilliant surgeon and, if the rumour was to be believed, a grandee of the Muslim Brotherhood. It was evident that he had a number of loyal followers involved in this plot and could obtain inside information – why target the Royal family? Airports and railways stations were much easier but, she supposed, the family rather than numbers had the bigger impact – a new line of terrorist thinking? Or was it part of a larger objective? Was this whole thing part of ISIL? She'd heard that they were the military wing of the Brotherhood.

Her knowledge of history wasn't too hot but to her it seemed like the many past wars of Muslims versus Christians.

At 0500 Callan relieved her; he was there for the next eight hours. She went home to have a bit of sleep, a shower and then back to the office to continue, taking over from Callan, checking on the group of unknowns.

She was still puzzling over the suspects when her mobile rang, it was Callan – the Russian was on the move and he needed instructions – it was 2pm. No, he said, she wasn't carrying anything and was wearing a red bomber jacket and blue jeans. She told him to follow keeping her posted on his mobile to say where he was. The Russian was heading north on the High Road. By the time she got there he'd lost her. At least they knew where she was hanging out, or thought they did.

Chapter
24

Five days to go

All of Gazelle's team needed to work out how they were going to get to the rendezvous without being followed. They needed to have the element of surprise when they arrived at Anmer.

Hammond's plan, along with his link man, was to pick up the Hovercraft and then camp on the beach near to Brancaster. To get to the barn where the craft was stored near Swaffham he would need to take a circuitous route.

He decided that he would drive to Swaffham and drop his link man off and drive on, his followers couldn't keep after both of them, especially so as the link man was going to take a cab, and whoever followed him would be on foot.

The link man would collect the Subaru with the Hovercraft. The followers were split up and Hammond would take his chance and drive out of Swaffham and head to Castle Acre. Heading north from there he would park his car by the Peddars Way and walk, with his camping equipment, north for about a mile, the link man would pick him up by a farmyard. He was pleased with his plan – he was ready for the off. He didn't know about the tracker on his car.

Deep in thought about his plan Gallagher was taken completely by surprise when a trout took his fly, it made him jump. He was on the hill with Trevor fishing for supper in a small loch – he got lucky with a two pound brown trout.

Lying on his back in the tent after a delicious supper of trout and whisky he was aware that he had no contingency plan, particularly with regard to the escape route, apart from that he was confident. Trevor was sound asleep. He decided he would go south by train, Trevor could drop him off at the station in Oban, the train would take him to Glasgow and then onto London.

What if the items in the barn were discovered he asked himself? He would tell Hammond to text him when he'd picked up the Hovercraft and to confirm all was okay at the barn. Hammond was going to be in Norfolk before him so if there was a problem he could put something else into place. He eventually fell into a deep sleep only to be wakened an hour later with torrential rain beating on the tent that was acting like a drum skin.

If the Russian got caught with the rifle, then the whole thing would have to be called off. This thought and the smell of frying bacon and coffee that Trevor was preparing for breakfast woke him. It was a fine morning.

Gallagher wasn't feeling communicative; he was going through the whole plot in his mind over and over. An idea came into his head from nowhere. He took his mobile from his breast pocket; he'd brought it with him through habit. There was a signal, a strong signal; they were about 1,200 feet up on the hill side. Walking away from the small camp it got even stronger. He rang an old contact in London who 'arranged' cars. He gave the specification of what he required and yes, it was possible to 'arrange' it in forty eight hours for £5,000. Cracked it, he said to himself.

After speaking to her boss Stone decided to get heavy with the manager of the club.

"Do you recognise this woman?" She held an image of the Russian.

148

"No."

"Then how come she came out of here at 2pm this afternoon?"

"I don't know."

"If that's the best you can do I'm going to have this place turned over."

He shrugged.

She rang Commander Tyson's office at the Yard and was about to ask for a team to be sent down to search the club when the manager said, "No, stop. Follow me."

After hanging up she followed the manager down to the cellars, it was dark and dingy. From what she could see it was previously the old stables of the 19ᵗʰ century building, there were two closed windows high up and one naked low watt light bulb. In the corner was a bucket, a camp bed with a sleeping bag and some clothing on top along with a cosmetics bag.

"Is this where she's staying?"

The manager nodded.

The place smelled really bad but she couldn't decide what the smell was. She poked around among the cobwebs and general muck - there was no sign of anything interesting. In the corner was a cupboard, about six foot tall and filthy, it could have been yellow or cream and it had a brand new expensive padlock; she was in two minds about forcing it open in front of the manager. The smell was overpowering, how could anyone sleep down here, she had to get outside.

Once in the street she rang Simmonds and told him what she'd found. She didn't know there was a rifle inside the cupboard but guessed there was.

"Don't open the cupboard and double up the surveillance, I need you back here so get Callan to organise it."

Four days to go

McLeod was on a conference call to her fellow heads.

"GCHQ is being swamped with warnings, so are our people on the ground. There are credible threats being made against us, in London, Manchester and Birmingham as well as Paris and Berlin, all security services are at breaking point. Someone is orchestrating this and we don't know who but suspect its ISIL.

"Curiously one of these threats is against the Duke of Cambridge at his Norfolk home. I say curiously because this was received by email, when checking the source, it came via one of our own servers here in London but we cannot trace where it originated. The message read - 20-23.6 Anmer assassination attempt."

"How can that happen Betine? What do you think it means?" asked Boswell.

"Our techs think someone with knowledge of our system has hacked into it to warn us. If it's genuine, and the consensus is that it is, then it looks like we have confirmation at last. But, as I understand it Max, we have nothing but circumstantial evidence against our group of suspects. Dare we risk letting this go ahead in the hope of netting a larger group, perhaps some of those at the very top?"

"We need specifics – is there anyway we can reach out to this person?" asked Simmonds.

"No. We've tried replying to the email but it bounces back and we've no idea where it came from geographically."

Stone was in Simmonds' office.

"Is it possible this person could be one of our suspects?" she asked generally, perhaps naively.

"Of course it's possible, but why do you ask?" responded McLeod. She sounded tetchy - clearly the strain was getting to her.

"I was thinking that if it is one of the suspects they would have to know the dates the Duke was going to be at Anmer. The only people apart from us and the palace to know the dates must be the assassin and their accomplices. The problem is which one sent the email. I'm sorry I was just thinking out loud."

"Don't be sorry Nat, I agree with you," said Simmonds. He continued. "Again we have three options. We can pull all the suspects in now, we know where they all live and work. I will ask the palace to cancel the Duke's visit and we all know we'll get short shrift from that, he'll say no way. Or we can let it run and get them in the act. I'll explain this to the PM and he can make the decision."

Having loaded his kit Trevor took Gallagher to Oban to catch the train in the rickety old 2CV; he only had to wait an hour. Once he'd made the connection in Glasgow he slept all the way to London; he couldn't care less about his ever present followers. They'd been waiting by the junction of the Glen Lonan/Oban road.

In London he kicked his heels for twenty four hours, then he called his contact about the vehicle. Yes, it would be ready in the morning, 11 am.

Three days to go

Gallagher got a cab from his King's Cross lodgings to Leytonstone. The cab, followed by the police, pulled into a disused railway yard. There was a row of railway arches with the fronts boarded in, each with a small door let into larger doors. The cab stopped by one with a board above the doors – Lenny's used motors.

Taking his bag and tripod tube he went through the smaller door, the police waited outside about 200 yards away. There, inside, was a pristine Ford Mondeo estate in Paramedic livery complete with blue lights. Having paid the £5,000 in cash he drove straight out of the other side of the arch and headed off for Norfolk. The police were still sitting there. Twenty minutes later they went in and asked where the man who had come in was. They were told he'd walked out of the other side of the arch. They'd well and truly lost him and had no idea what vehicle he was in. Gallagher's view was – always hide in plain sight, you're less likely to be noticed.

He got to his B&B in Harpley just as the pub was opening, it was 5pm; parking the car in the car park behind the pub he took his bag and booked in. The landlord who welcomed him said he thought he was in an ambulance that someone had called. Gallagher explained that he'd just bought the vehicle and was taking it to a man who'd been recommended to re-spray it. Relaxing with a pint of local ale he reflected that he'd lost the police and everything was looking good. He just needed to hear from Hammond about the barn.

Still no sign of the Russian but Stone was confident that all entrances into the club were covered. She was certain the rifle was in the cupboard and the suspect wouldn't be going anywhere without it.

Hammond was ready to go. He was collecting his link man from Colchester station at 08.45 in the morning.

Everyone else, apart from Gazelle and the Russian was in, or on their way to, Norfolk.

Chapter
25

Two days to go

Gazelle was feeling confident. Gallagher had everything under control and he was certain the operation would be a success. Being a vain man he wanted to be with his colleagues in the Brotherhood in Cairo when news of the successful assassination came through.

Having passed through security at Heathrow terminal 5 without a hitch he was heading toward the departure area when someone stepped in front him - it was a plain clothes police officer holding his warrant card in front of him. Just behind the Sheikh, on either shoulder, there were anti-terrorist officers with their carbines levelled.

"Sheikh Abdul Mohammed, you are under arrest for conspiring to carry out a terrorist act." He was given the usual caution. "Please come with us." The Sheikh said nothing. He was handcuffed and they left the building after the Sheikh's baggage was recovered.

Simmonds didn't think he could make the charge stick unless one of the other conspirators talked, but at least the Sheikh had been neutralised for the moment. First, cut the head off the snake was what he'd been taught. He now had fourteen days before he needed to formally charge him.

He'd been in touch with the Duke at the palace and he got the response he was expecting. The PM had agreed to let the plot work its way out and put a plan of his own regarding the Duke's security into place.

Hammond's idea worked perfectly until his link man took the cab in Swaffham, he looked out of the rear window as they drove off. The man following was writing something down, he presumed it was the number of the cab. The link man tried to call Hammond but had no signal on his mobile, a common problem in this part of the world.

Using their tracking system, the police eventually caught up with Hammond's car, parked by the Peddars Way – he'd gone, the car was empty, he could've been anywhere. A message came over their radio - the taxi driver had been found and had given the location of where he'd dropped off his fare from Swaffham. The driver punched the location into his sat-nav, it was in the rural hamlet of Narford, fifteen minutes away.

As arranged, Hamilton met up with his link man by the farmyard. He told him of his concerns about the policeman that had followed, no chances could be taken. They drove off in the Subaru with the Hovercraft on the trailer. Hammond began to gnaw at his fingernails again. They headed north and five minutes later he had had a signal.

Neither realised it, but he was passing the pub that Gallagher was staying in on the way to Brancaster. He told Gallagher what had happened and advised that no-one should go near the barn – Gallagher agreed and would notify all involved. He was pleased he'd taken the precaution of getting the other vehicle, the ambulance.

The police found the barn and after searching around found the padlock key under a breeze block about ten yards from the door. Inside was a motorbike and a Ford car, they touched neither but called in to request forensics on site. The owner of the barn said she'd been asked by an Irishman if he could rent it for 8 weeks and had paid cash in advance, the grain barn was not in use at this time of the year. No, she had no idea what was being stored, it was none of her business she said. The police would quickly discover the bike and Ford were both stolen.

Hammond arrived in Brancaster just after 6pm – the tide was out. They drove across the hard by the small harbour and took a small rough track above high water mark until they got to a little copse marked on their OS map. They parked up there, set up the two-man tent then started unloading the Hovercraft.

The trailer was of the flat-bed type and had a slide-out section under the main bed - this was slid out to form a ramp. Gallagher clambered up to the craft and started the engine, what a racket! He gingerly edged the craft forward, down the ramp and then switched off.

After getting their kit out of the Subaru they boarded the craft and set off toward the sea. They traversed the marsh in a veil of spray and continued to the still receding North Sea. They didn't know they were being watched but were certain that was the case as they roared back and forth until the light was starting to go – so far so good.

Still no sign of the Russian, Simmonds was getting an update from Stone. He told her they had arrested the Sheikh.

One day to go

Gallagher was thinking about his collection of the Russian from King's Lynn station in the morning, he had a change of plan; he needed to check something out but was certain she would be followed from London. It was a fine morning and the weather was set fair according to his landlord.

The paramedic vehicle didn't look at all out of place at the Queen Elizabeth hospital in King's Lynn. He parked alongside some ambulances, walked into the main entrance and sat in the waiting area observing people coming and going.

After looking at the floor plan he walked through the reception area, took the first right, then the first right again and continued to a door leading back outside. Okay, he thought to himself.

What he needed now was a dark green tunic to look like an authentic paramedic. As he walked past the parked ambulances he saw one on the seat of one of them, he reached through the open window and took it. With the tunic rolled up under his arm he walked around the back of the vehicle, the doors were open and it was empty, but there was a bright red blanket lying on the stretcher, he took that too.

He sent a text to the Russian to tell her that when she got to King's Lyn in the morning to take a cab to the hospital. When there, go through the main entrance, take the first right and right again, go to the end and he will be waiting outside. He knew her follower wouldn't be able to keep up without showing themselves.

After grabbing a sandwich at a garage he circumnavigated the Anmer estate to see if anything had changed. All was very quiet with nothing unusual going on; there was no sight of the familiar police Land Rovers. On the north east corner there were five bird watchers, their vehicles parked all higgledy-piggledy; the sight pleased him.

Back at Brancaster Hammond was attracting quite a crowd of holidaymakers with his antics in the Hovercraft; they were even applauding on occasions. The public had got used to seeing the craft.

Gallagher got back to his lodgings and ordered a pint which he took into the pub garden – that's it he said to himself, all done.

Chapter
26

20ᵗʰ June. Day One

Gazelle was not a happy man; he kept demanding his lawyer but was ignored. Fuming and apoplectic he wanted to know what the specific charge was, again he was ignored – let him sweat was Simmonds' instructions. The police were examining the Sheikh's baggage and mobile but so far had found nothing useful.

Simmonds got a call from Stone at 0600 to say that the Russian was on the move. She was following the taxi she'd taken from the club. The woman was wearing a striking, shocking pink top over blue jeans and white trainers; she was carrying a holdall and a gun slip – with her blonde hair she couldn't be missed. She followed the Russian to King's Cross and watched her board the 0645 King's Lynn train. After it left she telephoned her colleagues in Norfolk instructing them to follow the woman at that end.

As a precaution the Russian had got hold of a fake shotgun licence. Just as well because she was challenged by the ticket collector on the busy train. As suggested to her she told the collector she was on the way to a clay pigeon shoot near King's Lynn, he asked where and she said she didn't know, she was being picked up. It was unlikely he would check the inside of the slip and find a rifle rather than a shotgun. They got chatting and it turned out that he was a keen shooter too – truth was he fancied her like hell and was trying to pull.

The train emptied at Cambridge, as if someone had pulled the plug out. Half an hour later it drew into King's Lynn right on time. She had no difficulty in spotting the police as she walked to the cab rank; they followed in their car at a discreet distance while the cabbie drove to the hospital.

On the journey she'd agreed the fare and handed the driver a £20 note telling him to keep the change. They pulled up outside the main entrance and she got out and walked briskly into the hospital, following Gallagher's instructions to the letter – it worked. The one policeman waiting in his car not far behind Gallagher's had his vision blocked by an ambulance. The other policeman had no idea which way his suspect had gone when inside the hospital, he caught a glimpse of a pink top but when he got closer to the person he realised it was a man.

As soon as she got into the car she removed the pink top revealing a white T shirt tightly fitting across her large breasts. Then she put the rifle in the back covering it with the red blanket – it couldn't be seen. They were driving toward West Newton where they would turn right. She slipped on a pair of thorn-proof over trousers and a camouflage jacket; she had a forage cap and netting scarf in her hand.

Going past Sandringham and then onto Anmer, through the village with the Hall on the right they were approaching the crossroads, all was quiet. On the right, by the wood, there were half a dozen people, some were wearing camouflage and some with cameras on tripods, others looking south-east with binoculars – Twitchers.

Gallagher could see in his mirror a black Land Rover creeping along the lane, two police on board. They stopped, blocking the lane, and watched the group; Gallagher was the other side of the road. They watched for a few minutes, one of them on his radio – they paid no attention to Gallagher or his vehicle.

The junior of the two said, "Isn't that a bit strange, a paramedic vehicle being here Sarge?"

"Why, paramedics can be Twitchers too can't they?"

Eventually they drove off – it was 10.15am.

Several more birdwatchers drove up and parked haphazardly, they joined the others, some of their own team amongst them. Gallagher and the Russian got out and went over, Gallagher taking the black tripod tube case and the Russian the rifle with them. He put his camouflage jacket on and they stood around with the others. Altogether now there were around fifteen people and others were arriving.

The police returned, Gallagher glanced at his watch, 10.45am. They got out of the Land Rover and came over to the group - just as they were approaching someone, using that old childhood prank, said LOOK and pointed skywards. Gallagher, resisting the temptation, was watching – he knew there was nothing there. As he expected the police also looked up, that was his cue. He and the Russian slipped into the wood where they waited. Looking through the foliage they saw the police drive off five minutes later.

Before traversing the wood, he removed an aerosol from his pocket, it was the Capsaicin, they sprayed each other liberally, avoiding the eyes. If there were dogs around the spray should put them off any scent.

Shafts of sunlight were coming through the trees like sunbeams. The woodland floor was overgrown and combined with the dense tree canopy it was very gloomy in places. They stopped, about half-way across the wood, and listened – nothing. The Russian, without saying anything, had spotted a movement sensor strapped to a tree, she pointed at it. Gallagher looked, the tell-tale light was off - it was disarmed.

Just before the far edge of the wood they stopped by a huge Ash tree, they would have been invisible from outside the wood in the bright sunlight. They both got onto the prone position and the Russian slid the rifle from its slip. With their binoculars they studied the scene in front of them, overlooking the house, gardens and swimming pool - there was no-one around. The wood was about 80 feet above sea level, their position was perfect according to the Russian – height was an advantage. She still had no idea who the target was or, indeed, where she was. It was 10.58am.

Preparing the rifle, she found a relatively firm piece of ground and lowered the integral tripod, checked the sighting, loaded a cartridge clip and pronounced she was ready.

They waited. It was getting hot and sultry under the tree canopy – a bit like the jungle she thought. Now noon and there was still no activity. They each had a small bottle of water that was now warm, not thirst quenching. It was as if the Hall was deserted and all the police had gone home – nothing. Gallagher sensed this was a tactic. Either their intelligence was flawed or the police were waiting for him to make the first move. A Roe deer wandered across the line of sight of the rifle and the Russian took aim, as if she was about to fire. It was really hot now. The swimming pool, glistening in the sunlight, looked particularly inviting.

The rifle was sprayed with the Capsaicin and buried in the undergrowth. They raked around the area they had been with twigs to make sure there were no signs of their presence. Both had been trained not to leave traces.

They cautiously made their way through the wood not sure what to expect when they got back to their starting point, it was 2.30pm. There were only three people there. Apparently the police had just left; none of those remaining were Gallagher's team.

He'd taken the precaution of booking another room for the Russian at the pub just in case, but before going there he wanted to drive around the estate – it was strangely quiet. They passed several gamekeepers in their green John Deere mules going about their business, but no police. When he'd found a spot with a mobile signal he called the boat charter company. Yes, everything was okay and they would repeat their actions tomorrow. He then sent a prearranged text to the team – Repeat

Tomorrow. They got back to the pub and enjoyed a thirst quenching drink.

Ned Boswell had stationed himself in the Hall. He and one of his officers took turns at a first floor window scanning the countryside around the Hall with powerful binoculars they saw nothing suspicious.

The only activity, according to his radio reports were bloody birdwatchers, he wanted them out of the way but there was nothing he could do about it. He was beginning to wonder if they'd got it wrong. There were armed undercover officers all around the house but no-one had seen anything apart from the birdwatchers.

He changed shifts at 6pm; positions would be maintained throughout the night. He'd thought about the wood on the horizon but dismissed it as being too far away, and no movement had been observed - nearly a mile away he estimated. They had police on the far side of the wood keeping an eye on the birdwatchers. Nonetheless he wanted it swept before dusk – dog teams were called in but nothing was found. The Duke and Duchess had been delayed; they were going to arrive by helicopter early in the morning.

"We've found some numbers on the Sheikh's mobile that are in Egypt," the techie was telling Simmonds. "There are three numbers in particular that he calls regularly. I've contacted the security service in Cairo and they checked. One of the numbers is the Sheikh's sister, another is the main hospital in Cairo and the third is a judge that they think is a senior member of the Muslim Brotherhood. You're not going to like this sir, but Cairo knows we have the Sheikh locked up."

"What! How the hell do they know that?" He was red with rage, furious.

Chapter
27

21st June. Day Two

Midsummer's day - a fine one at that.

Gallagher and the Russian turned up earlier than the day before - they were by the wood just before 10am. There was a much larger crowd, about forty people. A sea eagle had been seen twenty minutes earlier - like a flying barn door as someone described it. There were two police Land Rovers present, the occupants watching the avian enthusiasts.

It wasn't necessary for anyone to call out LOOK, but they did anyway; there was plenty of cover from the growing crowd to enable them to slip away unnoticed. They went about twenty yards and stopped, listening. Apart from the murmur of the birdwatchers it was silent. They sprayed each other with the pepper concentrate before moving off.

Simmonds had a call from the Home Office about the Sheikh, the Egyptians were demanding his immediate release - a diplomatic row was brewing. He wasn't the greatest diplomat and was keen to tell them to bugger off but, self preservation and responsibility told him otherwise.

Stone was still researching the people that had been on the plane when she came across an article in the New York Times on the internet about a Sultan Ahmed Mohammed. The name is common in Arabia, but she thought it worth reading.

It was dated ten years ago and concerned the trial of this Sultan in Cairo. He had been charged with conspiracy to overthrow the government of Hosni Mubarak. One of the key witnesses for his defence was the then head of the Egyptian secret service, the Mukhabarat. Strangely, it was them that made the accusation in the first place. The charge was dropped and he was released. The image accompanying the article was non-descript, it supposedly showed the Sultan in Arab dress.

The article went on to give some biographical information about the Sultan that included the fact that he had been at Oxford, she guessed, at the same time as Simmonds and McLeod, they were all of a similar age. He trained as a surgeon in London. His sultanate was subsumed by Egypt in his fathers' day but he still had much respect and influence in state affairs. This had to be their Sheikh.

She was summoned to a meeting by Simmonds. McLeod was there, a minister from the Home Office and another from the Foreign Office. Both Offices were being pressured by the Egyptian government to release the suspect and allow him to return to Cairo. Stone sat silently turning over in her mind what this new information meant, it certainly posed some potentially difficult questions.

It was incredibly humid and large clouds were bubbling up in the west. Before they'd gone another couple of hundred yards the rain started to rattle on the leaves, a clap of thunder and then it was pouring. They were getting some shelter from the trees but it was looking like the day was going to be a washout.

They got into position by the Ash tree; it was just before 11am, the rifle was left buried. They could see some activity in the Hall through the driving rain, but Gallagher thought it unlikely the Duke, if he was there, would be going swimming. He was right - the Duke was playing with his children in the nursery, he'd arrived earlier that morning.

Gallagher had to make a decision, does he call the whole thing off, or try again in the morning. They made their way back to find that only

164

two people were still peering through their binoculars and braving the weather. There were no police present.

Pretty wet after their excursion they drove off to find somewhere more secluded to send text messages. The Russian knew she had to get a result to get the balance of her fee so agreed to have another go tomorrow. He sent a text to all concerned asking for an urgent response. The boat charter company was called and they were on for tomorrow provided they were paid in advance as they had been to date.

Slowly but surely the text replies started to come in, without exception they were all okay for tomorrow. They then drove to Brancaster to pay the boat charter company for tomorrow. It was only noon so they went and had some lunch then drove into King's Lynn to watch a film killing time.

Boswell was looking out of the first floor window through the torrential rain. He hadn't seen any activity and nothing unusual had been reported, he came to the same conclusion as Gallagher but warned his officers to stay on high alert.

"How realistic is it that your case will stand up in a court Max?" asked the Home Office official, John Willsher."

"I take it that everyone in this room is familiar with Operation Jonah?" he looked around the room - everyone nodded. "A plot to assassinate the Duke is underway as we speak, to make a charge against the Sheikh stick we have to round up the rest of his team in the act so to speak. Otherwise a half decent lawyer will get him off. My guess is that he is the top man and will, in time, lead us to others, if we let him go now, when we can legally detain him, he will disappear."

"From what I can see we have no evidence and it might be seen that we are misusing the terrorism act. Apart from that we have a major trade deal going down with the Egyptians right now and we don't want to jeopardise that do we," said Willsher in a patronising way.

Stone didn't know what to do. The thought of compromising her boss with the new found information horrified her, but who could she turn to?

"What do your people in Cairo have to say?" said Simmonds. This was directed at McLeod.

"Nothing more than we already know."
It was agreed they should make the Egyptians wait until the morning.

The meeting broke up and it was just Simmonds, McLeod and Stone left, the latter asked to speak - she started by apologising.

"I'm very sorry but I think you should both see this article." She handed them copies of the New York Times piece. They read. They both looked puzzled.

"Good Lord, I haven't seen him for about thirty years. Do you remember him at Oxford Betine?"

"Vaguely, I think he was doing medicine wasn't he, I didn't see much of him, just at the Union debates. I don't recognise him from this image though."

"I remember him in those debates, bit of an extremist I seem to recall. Why are you showing us this Nat?"

"Because he is the same man that we are holding, the Sheikh - of that I'm certain."

"I don't recognise that at all Nat, I'm sure I would have remembered his golden locks."

"Ah, but if you think back Max, he always wore an Arab headdress and a suit, the headdress had a snazzy red and white securing cord," said McLeod.

"So our man's a Sultan is he…. a lot of clout."

"Yes Max, we should tread carefully."

Stone was relieved, it all seemed innocent to her.

Gallagher was getting nervous about using the paramedic vehicle for a third day in a row. He decided to go into nearby Fakenham first thing in the morning, and, using yet another of his fake licences, hire a nondescript car. He would leave his present one in a supermarket car park.

Hammond had been rained off too. He and his link man decided to spend the day in a local pub and got thoroughly plastered, well Hammond did but his link man was teetotal.

Come 6pm the rain stopped and the sun came out, the forecast was good.

Chapter
28

22nd June. Day three

By 9.30am they'd got the hire car and driven immediately to Anmer arriving there before 10am – there was no-one about. They parked away from the wood and walked back to it unobserved in the sparsely populated village, they entered and when about half-way across stopped and listened.

There was clear evidence that dogs had been through the wood recently, the Russian was standing in it – she swore under her breath, in Russian Gallagher assumed as he suppressed a snigger.

Apart from birdsong they could hear nothing until two sets of car doors slammed in succession, they waited. As the muffled tones of Twitchers drifted toward them they sprayed themselves with the pepper and continued. They belly crawled the last thirty or so yards to where the rifle had been buried, it hadn't been disturbed. They were conscious that it was earlier in the morning and the light was penetrating further into the wood.

Leaving the rifle for the moment they shuffled into position by the Ash tree. Looking down into the natural amphitheatre there he was. They raised their binoculars in unison. The figure was semi-reclining in a sun-lounger next to the pool, there were drying footprints leading to the lounger.

The Russian crawled back to the rifle and exhumed it before returning to the Ash tree, Gallagher hadn't moved, he was still surveying the scene.

"That's your target," he said to the Russian.

She picked up her binoculars again to study the figure on the lounger. He was wearing a wet, Edwardian style horizontal striped single piece full-body swimsuit; many men still wore this style on the Black Sea she reflected. He appeared to be dozing after a swim as his eyes were closed, his hands held an open book in his lap. By his side was a crumpled towel and small table with a cup on it, empty, as she could see through the powerful scope with crystal clarity– no-one else was present.

"Head or chest?"

It could have been either, but the lounger had a shade that cast a slight shadow over the head.

"Chest," she said.

She put on a pair of Latex gloves before unhurriedly removing the slip from the rifle and setting the rifle up. As she was adjusting the scope Gallagher nudged her.

"There's someone coming." He said sotto voce.

Peripheral vision through the scope is non existent so she didn't spot the woman appearing to tip-toe gingerly across the terrace. Clearly she didn't want to disturb the Duke; it must have been a maid as she was there to collect the empty cup.

It was getting very hot under the tree canopy and they were both perspiring, there was no wind to deflect the bullet so windage adjustment was unnecessary she was thinking to herself.

"Ready?" he asked.

"Da," she responded in her native tongue as she inserted the ammunition clip into the breech of the rifle.

She pulled the bolt back and then pushed it forward to put the first bullet into the chamber. Audibly she took a deep breath, steadied herself as a trained professional would and, after a moments pause squeezed the trigger very gently.

Three sharp cracks in quick succession. Gallagher was watching. Very close grouping, all around the heart. The victim's head fell forward and one of the hands holding the book fell down by the side of the lounger, blood was spreading across the striped swimsuit – there was no movement. It was a strange feeling to be so far away, a sense of total detachment, as if watching a film.

The Russian started to shuffle backwards but Gallagher restrained her by the wrist. "Wait!" he hissed.

He wasn't concerned about the three sharp cracks, he'd learned that rifle and shotgun shots were commonplace around the area at all times of the year – either game shooting or culling of one sort or another. Until the body was examined and the area searched no-one would know from which direction the shots had come from.

It took only moments before people started to appear on the terrace and start running toward the pool. First on the scene was a shirt sleeved police officer, he knelt down and looked for a pulse before getting on his radio, within a minute sirens started screeching. Gallagher was satisfied.

They left the rifle and walked calmly back to the edge of the wood and took up positions with their binoculars, standing with a group of about ten bird watchers. Within a couple of minutes of arriving two unmarked police vehicles, a Land Rover and a Ford, went hurtling past with sirens blaring.

Unbeknown to Gallagher and the Russian the police were on their way to set up a road block on the crossroads – the same was being done at all junctions around the Hall, no-one could get through.

After a couple of minutes, they casually walked back to the car hand-in-hand, initially she had objected to this but he persuaded her for appearance sake. Binoculars swinging from their necks it would all have looked perfectly innocent to any observers, but there weren't any.

As they got to the car they could hear a helicopter but couldn't see it. Was it the air ambulance he asked himself? They only drove for about two hundred yards before turning off onto a narrow farm track by the village sign, it was an unmade road but the Vauxhall coped with it. There were hundreds of these tracks in this part of the world he'd discovered, many not marked on the OS map. He had done a number of dummy runs and was now familiar with this particular route.

Back in London Simmonds was in live radio contact with Ned Boswell at Anmer, it was a secure link. There was a further link to the Prime Minister's office. It was swarming with police at Anmer; they had put up large screens around the pool and terrace area keeping prying eyes out. Behind the screens the body was being removed and the area cleaned up leaving no traces of what had happened. Under the Prime Minister's orders, a press curfew was in place – this would remain for some time; everyone involved had been sworn to absolute secrecy.

Under extreme pressure from two government departments Simmonds was forced to release the Sultan, but not before a message had been received on his mobile – Completed –G. This still was not enough in itself to get a conviction. The Sultan was now on his way to Heathrow.

The tip off received had been accurate but they were no further forward. They'd lost Gallagher and the Russian as well as Hammond, and the Sultan was on his way back to Egypt. How can these people disappear into thin air? Simmonds asked himself.

Gallagher and the Russian bumped along the dusty potholed track until they reached the main road in Great Bircham, here they had to halt as there was a steady flow of traffic heading for the coast. By pure chance one of the cars contained Stone and she spotted Gallagher for the second time, waiting at the T junction he didn't see her. She was with Fiona on their way to Brancaster for lunch. There wasn't much she could do in London and had gone up to Great Massingham to be closer to the action.

Flipping the vanity mirror on the passenger side down she told Fiona to continue. Watching Gallagher's Vauxhall in the mirror and using her mobile at the same time was tricky, she was trying to call her boss but there was no signal. She saw the car pull out and much to her relief it turned in their direction.

There was a fork in the road coming up and Fiona asked what she should do. To the right the road to the Burnhams, to the left the road to Brancaster, she told her to go left. Gallagher, six cars behind, came the same way. Just outside Docking she got a signal on the mobile and called Simmonds.

"No I haven't got a registration number but it's a dark blue Vauxhall Corsa. There's a blonde female passenger, I think it's the Russian woman. We are just outside the village of Docking heading toward the coast. We're in a white Saab convertible with the roof down."

"Hang on - I'm going to get a helicopter scrambled. Well done Nat."

"Thank you sir."

172

There was a long pause; she could hear him on another telephone, then she lost the signal.

"Bloody Norfolk!"

Fiona laughed - she didn't have a clue what this was all about.

Stone could only follow her instincts; it's what she'd been trained to do.

"Carry on for Brancaster and let's hope he follows"

At the crossroads Fiona did a right and then a left and he did the same. He was now only two cars behind.

The mobile rang twice and then stopped, it was a weak signal.

About a mile clear of Docking there was another fork in the road.

"I normally go right up here Nat – what do you want me to do?"

"Pull over and let him pass and we'll follow him."

The blue Vauxhall along with four other cars passed, they all forked right. They set off again, this time behind.

Simmonds, unable to contact Stone was tearing his hair out when his radio-phone bleeped, it was the police controller at Sculthorpe airfield - the helicopter had a visual on the white Saab; it was in a line of five cars nearing Brancaster Hall. The only part of Stones message that was clear was white Saab convertible and Docking, the police had done well to find it.

Rounding the 90 degree bend in front of the Hall driveway everyone had to pull over on the single track road to let a tractor coming the other way pass – it didn't matter as no-one seemed to be in a hurry, a bit different to London Stone was thinking.

After clearing the bend there was another fork in the road. Three cars went straight on and they and the Vauxhall went left across the Heath and down the hill to the Jolly Sailors pub. Police cars, some marked and some unmarked were all converging on the area, the helicopter still had visual.

At the junction Stone could see she had a full signal on her mobile.

"Right or left?" asked Fiona.

She didn't know.

They turned right and followed the Vauxhall to the harbour.

"Is there another way out?"

"No."

The mobile rang, at last a clear signal. It was Simmonds. She told Fiona to stop just where they were.

"Sorry sir the signal around here is terrible. We're in a village called Brancaster, the suspect has just driven to the harbour – what do you want me to do?"

"I know exactly where you are, we have a helicopter watching you and the cavalry are on the way."

The harbour area was a pretty spot and a hive of activity, holidaymakers everywhere. It was a fine afternoon with the sea flat calm. Gallagher and the Russian were getting out of the Vauxhall, they went to the boot and he took out a grip and handed it to her, there was no sign of a rifle she reported.

They walked across the poorly kept potholed car park toward a slipway where a launch was sitting on an ebbing tide, Neptune was its name. The Russian boarded it, the throttles were pushed forward, the stern dug in and it went off she told Simmonds. The driver wanted to clear the sand bar at the mouth of the harbour before the tide exposed it.

"Okay, I've got that and I'm passing it to the Coastguards to keep an eye on it. What else can you see?"

"I'm just watching Gallagher; he's gone to a sandwich kiosk. It's very busy here, so many boats around the place. Okay, he's got a snack and he's walking across the car park but..........not towards his car. He's approaching ....I can't quite see what it is, there's a crowd of people around it. From what I can see it's bright red........and it reminds me of those things they use in the swamps of the Everglades in America.............." She craned her neck further. "No....... its some sort of Hovercraft."

"What is he doing?"

"I can't see, just looking I suppose, like a lot of others.........no, hang on, I think that's Hammond as well and one of the other guys on the plane."

"At last," said Simmonds. "We've got them all in one place, wait there and do not move."

Just then there was an enormous roar as the Hovercraft started up, dust, sand, dirt and spray flew everywhere as it pulled away, there were three occupants; all the holidaymakers had turned their backs to the craft trying to avoid the flying debris. It set off in a Northerly direction skimming across a mix of marsh and sea.

Chapter
29

The Coastguard had picked up the launch Neptune on radar, it was heading into Wells harbour, there would be a reception committee waiting for the Russian when it arrived.

Concerned that she might be stopped the Russian had hidden the balance of her fee, £40,000, in the seat cushions of the Neptune; she planned on returning to collect it at a later stage. It was found by Neptune's owners some months later and they handed it into the police. No-one claimed it and it was given back to them six months later.

Simmonds still had an open line to the PM who was listening intently. He was also juggling with the line to the police helicopter and Stone.

After the Hovercraft had departed he told her to stand down for the time being. The helicopter was keeping its distance but shadowing the craft; that is until it reported it was running dangerously short of fuel and had to return to Sculthorpe. Its last sighting of the craft was just off Hunstanton, it appeared to be heading across the Wash toward Lincolnshire, a distance of about 20 miles to the nearest shore at Freiston.

He knew his job and reputation were on the line here, he mustn't lose the suspects again - they had to be caught at all costs.

There was a brief interchange between Simmonds and the Prime Minister then the link was terminated. Less than a minute later his mobile rang, it was the Station Commander at RAF Marham, Wing Commander Jacks.

"I've been instructed to contact you Mr Simmonds by the Ministry of Defence - how can I help you?"

"Good Lord - that was quick, thank you Wing Commander. We have a little difficulty with some suspected terrorists trying to evade us by crossing the Wash in a Hovercraft and wonder if you can help to stop them."

"I should think so. I've been instructed to give you every assistance including the use of lethal force if necessary. We have two sorties in the air at present, Tornado GR4 aircraft. They are on bombing practice at Holbeach and I can divert them if you so wish."

"That would be most helpful. If you find the suspects, please shake them up for me. Their craft is red and has three occupants; they were last seen off Hunstanton fifteen minutes ago. We will be trying to get police in place on the other shore but, of course, we don't know their exact destination, please keep me informed of their course."

He wished he could be there. There was no need to define 'shake up', he would leave that to the pilots.

The RAF bombing range at Holbeach and the Wash in general has been used for dummy bombing and strafing practice for many years; usually it was the merchant shipping that were the unsuspecting targets, sometimes naval craft were involved too.

The Wash is a dangerous and unpredictable stretch of water, very deep in places and with treacherous, continuously moving sandbanks, rip tides are common.

The four Tornados approached line astern from the south west, the sun directly behind them at, in RAF parlance, zero feet. The passengers on the craft couldn't have seen or heard the aircraft until they arrived. They 'attacked' in pairs at several hundred miles per hour totally surprising the 'enemy'.

The turbulent jet wake, the shockwave and the unbelievable noise shook the craft and its occupants, it was designed to terrify them - the effects were similar to a stun grenade. They saw stars and lost all sense of awareness for a couple of moments.

Before they could recover there was a repeat performance. This time the craft almost capsized tipping one of the passengers into the sea, it circled and the fortunate soul was dragged back aboard. He was lucky as the notorious currents were pulling the vessel out to sea on the ebbing tide. Their course was now erratic, zigzagging all over the sea like a drunken cork.

The pilot of the lead Tornado left it for the moment - he wanted the suspects to think their ordeal was all over, they were about 8 miles from the Lincolnshire shore, nearly there they could see the old Freiston coastal artillery searchlight tower on the horizon.

Three minutes later, out of nowhere again they 'attacked'. This time the Hovercraft did capsize decanting the hapless terrorists into the cold North Sea.

The squadron leader in command of the sortie radioed for emergency assistance giving the GPS coordinates. Within minutes the Hunstanton lifeboat, ironically a Hovercraft, was on its way. The Humberside air/sea rescue helicopter was also scrambled. A lone Tornado, circled the scene, the others had returned to RAF Marham.

All three occupants were clinging to the upturned hull of the craft which was rapidly being washed further out to sea; none appeared to be wearing a life vest and two were, even at 500 feet, clearly struggling to hang on as the fierce current dragged at their legs. The ETA of the helicopter was 4 minutes, the lifeboat 15 minutes.

One of the passengers lost his hand-hold and was swept away at a surprising rate of knots, his arms feebly flailing for a moment and then he was gone, under the waves to his watery grave. The Tornado pilot was helpless; he couldn't do anything but watch. He was in the silent world of his cockpit, detached as Gallagher had been when the assassin fired her rifle.

Just as the helicopter was approaching another let go of the craft to succumb to the same fate as his companion, there was nothing anyone could do to save him.

The helicopter winch man just managed to grab the sole survivor as he let go of the craft on the edge of consciousness. The pilot headed for the nearest medical centre, the crew giving first-aid as they went. When the lifeboat arrived a few minutes later they started a search of the area, a search the crew's experience told them would be fruitless. After three hours they returned empty handed to Hunstanton with the other vessel in tow. It had been impressed upon the RAF and the emergency services that no-one could talk to the media in any form.

The nearest hospital that could cope with the rescue helicopter was King's Lynn. The sole survivor was suffering from extreme hypothermia and couldn't be interviewed by the police; two armed officers were left on guard outside his single bed ward. The occupant was Wolfe Dean, aka Hammond.

An unmarked black Mercedes panel van was parked behind Anmer Hall - it had a refrigeration unit on the roof. Two men were at the rear, one was locking the van's door – both men were in their early fifties and wearing a white short sleeve shirt with black tie and black trousers, they looked sombre.

The vehicle was driven slowly down the drive until it reached an inordinately large oak five-bar gate; there wasn't the usual magic eye to open it. Instead there was a camera perched on a pole fifty feet above the ground; it revolved, scanning the vicinity before there was a clunk, the operating mechanism for the gate, it opened slowly outwards. They were on their way to Addenbrookes Hospital in Cambridge.

They pulled up outside the mortuary, a discreet unmarked building behind the hospital. Here they unloaded a body bag onto a stretcher and wheeled it into the building, after checking in the bag it was signed for by an orderly. They were returning a cadaver 'borrowed' by MI5 two days earlier. The body, donated for medical science, was that of a man in his mid-thirties who had tragically died from a brain tumour. The cadaver was in good condition apart from three black holes around the heart.

Preparation of the cadaver to resemble the Duke was carried out by a mortician, an undertaker and a make-up artist, the Duke's contribution was his treasured striped single piece swimsuit, if the swimsuit became public knowledge it would start a craze. Beneath the swimsuit a blood bag was taped to the torso. Rigor mortis was long gone so the body was flexible.

Ned Boswell had no idea when the assassin would strike, maybe he or she wouldn't. They only had the tip-off to go on.

The Duke's arrival was delayed. The next day he arrived, along with the cadaver, it poured with rain. On the third day they started early in the morning, the forecast was good so the cadaver was arranged and the props set up, including the puddles by the lounger. Every hour on the hour the 'maid' would collect the empty cup – it was like amateur dramatics but, it was the PM's idea and nobody had a better one. For all they knew they were being watched, as it happened they weren't. The ruse paid off but, they didn't have any idea of where the three shots came from.

Extensive woodland covers three sides of the estate and it was impossible to police all of it, if they'd tried the suspects would have been frightened off. The road blocks didn't work and if it wasn't for the sharp eyed Nat Stone they would have been at a complete loss as to where the perpetrators were. After drafting in even more police and dogs to search the woods the rifle and spent cartridges were eventually found but, there were no fingerprints.

Chapter
30

The PM was seeking assurances that the threat to the life of the Duke was over. It wasn't in Simmonds' nature to commit over such an issue; you never knew what was around the corner, besides there were still unanswered questions. But he did say, more than likely. The PM seemed satisfied

Exhausted, he'd fallen asleep. It was 11am and the telephone conversation had lasted nearly an hour. When it had finished he put his head on his arms on the desk and that was it – he was undisturbed for forty minutes or so then the phone started ringing again, it never ended. He wanted time to think and close the book on the Duke's case.

He had a doctor's appointment in the afternoon, with no sleep last night he was concerned that he had been under the weather for about a month now and it was getting worse. Pretty certain his doctor would say it was his work load he needed to get that confirmed.

The debriefing meeting was scheduled for 12.30. Attached to his office was a small apartment, he was thinking perhaps a broom cupboard might be a better description. It's where he would sleep when there was an emergency on; he'd spent the last five nights there. It comprised a single bed that he kept meaning to do something about, it was desperately uncomfortable, a shower, loo and washbasin, all very primitive. He took his second shower of the day then had a strong coffee - it didn't make him feel any better.

It was the usual group that met in that soulless room at Thames House.

"I hope you don't mind but I've invited Nat to this meeting as she was instrumental in tracking our terrorist cell and has shown to be invaluable to operation Jonah."

McLeod and Boswell showed their approval by giving Stone a handclap, a tradition in the service. She blushed.

"I'm pretty certain we foiled this plot to assassinate the Duke and I want to know what you all think – Betine, over to you."

"I agree. However, do we know who masterminded the operation Max? Whoever it was has mind far more sophisticated than the type we normally come up against. I think that is evident in the pre-planning."

"What about you Ned?"

"Betine is right, my moneys on this Gallagher bloke but, we'll never know as he's dead, well at least we think he's dead. Is it possible anyone could have survived those waters? I wouldn't put anything past this guy,"

"That's a very good question Ned. We really don't know anything about him so it's impossible to speculate, but I guess an exceptional swimmer might be able to do it. Nat, can you make some enquiries to see if there's a record of anyone swimming the width of the Wash?"

"Sorry sir, but I anticipated this was where you were going and I've done some brief research."

"Good God Nat, you never cease to amaze me, well done. Go on."

"The most improbably named Miss Mercedes Gleitz was the first recorded. She swam the Wash on the 20th June 1929, it took her thirteen and a quarter hours. More recently someone called Murphy in 1973; Spry in 1974 and Read, three times in 1974/5/6. There's even a trophy for the achievement."

The other three looked astounded.

"So it is possible," said Simmonds. "Hmm........ maybe you are right Ned. According to the RAF he would only have to have swum around another 8 miles to reach the shore. I imagine, if he made it, he'd have been pretty exhausted. Nat, we'd better not take any chances, get onto Lincolnshire police and get some of our people up there straight away, if he's there someone must have seen him."

Stone left the room.

"That girl's brilliant Max, don't lose her, she's going far," said McLeod.

"Now the tally. We just don't know about the Sultan, and I don't think we ever will, he's gone anyway. Hammond, well, all we have on him is driving around Balmoral in a vehicle purchased from a spurious source and trying to evade the authorities, we don't have anything that will stick. Do we agree that he should be released without charge but flagged as a terrorist associate?"

The other two nodded their assent.

"That just leaves the Russian. She swears she was holidaying in the UK and met Gallagher in Norfolk, a load of rubbish, but the only evidence we have is circumstantial. Yes, she is ex Russian army and yes, the rifle found at Anmer was Russian but there were no fingerprints; and yes, we have her photographed with the Sultan but none of that will get us a conviction. Unless you disagree I will recommend deportation.

"Without a body we're not sure who the other guy was that we think drowned. Nat is certain he was one of those on the aircraft but doesn't know which one. Until we can come to a conclusion about Gallagher the case has to remain open but, apart from him, I think we've now identified and placed all the main suspects."

There was knock on the door, Stone came in.

"Sir, we're very short staffed at the moment due to holidays. Would it be alright if I went up to Lincolnshire, I'm the only person who can identify him first hand? The local police think he'll have come ashore around the remote village of Freiston a couple of miles east of Boston, they are doing a house-to house and have set up road blocks in a twenty mile arc of the shore."

It was a long journey but the weather was gorgeous so she decided to take the Norton. She caught a cab to Walthamstow, donned her leathers, grabbed an overnight bag, started the bike and she was on her way weaving through the traffic heading north.

The traffic was awful when she got to King's Lynn and it got worse on the A17. To make matters worse she got hopelessly lost after Boston. Managing to find the only pub in Freiston by the Church, The Kings Head, it had taken her nearly five hours from London. A sleepy, little village; the funny little pub was entered by a red door - she went in, it was like stepping back in time - no-one there. She called out, no answer. As she stepped outside a police patrol car with two occupants pulled up.

"Can we help miss?" asked the driver in a friendly manner.

"I hope so. I'm looking for two things, accommodation and your officer in charge," she said with a winning smile on her pretty face. She had reservations about the Lincolnshire police after the cock-up in following suspects from the airport before.

They were both out of the car now, the younger one clearly fancied himself in that swaggering way that youngster's in uniform often do.

"You won't find any here they don't have rooms, there's a guest house down the road," he said pointing, "about half a mile, in Freiston Shore. Why do you want to see the officer in charge?"

She was irritated by his manner.

"Never you mind, just tell me where I can find them please."

"I'll deal with this Jake," said the older one.

"I'll call him up miss - do you mind telling me who you are?"

"My name is Natalie Stone from MI5," she said presenting her ID.

Their jaws dropped open simultaneously. She loved it.

Mounting the bike she rode off to the guest house - Inspector Barton said he would meet her there. It was a strange part of the world, the like of which she'd never seen - slightly eerie.

The guest house in the tiny hamlet of Shore was just a short distance, about 100 yards, from the Wash, Norfolk was visible on the other side; she wondered if the three properties she could see flooded. The door of the guest house was opened by a woman in her fifties, yes she could have a room she was told in a reserved manner; it was £20 a night including breakfast.

Having checked in she quickly took of her leathers, asked for a glass of water, she was gasping, and took it the bench in front of the house where she waited for the Inspector; it was a fine early evening.

Sitting there in the sun in T shirt and jeans she was reflecting on the daunting prospect of swimming 8 miles of the empty stretch of the Wash in front of her, let alone the whole width; 14 hours in that freezing water beggars belief. It looked calm enough at the moment but the currents that lurked below the surface were known to be extremely powerful. Nothing was stirring; she'd heard the expression before but had never experienced it – the sound of silence.

She was miles away when the unmarked black Ford pulled up outside the guest house. A tall man in his forties got out. He was wearing a white shirt with epaulettes bearing two pips indicating he was a police inspector.

"Miss Stone?" he enquired.

"Yes, Inspector Barton?"

"Good evening, Miss Stone could I please see your ID."

She handed it to him and he studied it closely before handing it back. He was quite good looking she was thinking.

"May I?" he asked as he joined her on the bench. She nodded.

He unfolded the map he was carrying and pointed to the areas that had been searched.

"It's very sparsely populated around here, mostly farms, farmworker's cottages and plenty of outbuildings, all of those in the area have been searched but nothing has been found. People around here are not very communicative and no-one has seen any strangers in the area recently, whether or not they would tell us if they had is another matter."

"How likely do you think it is that our man could have swum 8 miles to get here?"

"I think it's quite possible, it's been done before. I've just had a call from the coastguard at Bridlington and he has re-checked the tides, he now thinks we should be looking further north east, I've just been getting the road blocks moved. We are now going to centre the search south of Skegness. I am just going to the village of Fiskney, we're setting up the incident room there – would you like to come with me?"

They caught up with and followed the police mobile incident room into Fiskney, another, small remote village on the banks of the Wash, the landscape all around as flat as a pancake under enormous skies. She was thinking it must be a depressing place in the depths of winter.

She waited in the car studying the OS map while the inspector gave his instructions; then they went on a tour of the road blocks.

By now it was nearly 9pm but still broad daylight. More police were arriving at dawn from the south Yorkshire force - the locals simply couldn't cope with searching the vast area on their own. She left her mobile number on the car's dashboard and asked to be dropped at the pub in Freiston, she was starving. The inspector apologised, saying time hadn't moved on around there, "it's still chicken in a basket I'm afraid, but it is edible - just!"

The pub was busy and all the locals gawked at her when she entered, intimidating, she ignored it. After steak and chips with a half of cider she walked back to the guest house and crashed out – before he dropped her off she agreed to meet the inspector at the incident room at 8am in the morning.

Chapter
31

There were now around 120 people involved in the search over a wide area. It was 11.30am and the house to house of the small number of properties was complete, it was a zero.

Along the shores of the Wash, on both sides, there are many derelict WW2 defences including a chain of pill boxes, the machine guns long since removed. In one of these a searcher found evidence that someone had been there recently. There were egg shells scattered around and evidence of a fire, not very conclusive and the place was full of rubbish but he radioed it in anyway.

Stone was on the point of calling the search off when the call came into the incident room. She was sitting with the inspector drinking coffee and poring over a large scale map of the area.

"Where?" He looked at the map and, after a pause said "I'm on my way, be with you in ten minutes - don't touch anything."

He and Stone raced off in the black Ford. They couldn't get any closer than a field entrance, then it was a 200 yard walk down a rough track to get to the pill box with a policeman standing beside it.

The inspector switched his torch on and peered inside, apart from the rubbish the stench was awful; Stone had a look too. Yes, there were egg shells on the floor and a rough bed made of cardboard in one corner, but no indication as to who or when someone was there, the little heap of ashes were cold. They agreed it was doubtful they would be able to recover any fingerprints from the site.

They both looked toward the water about 80 yards away in the hope that footprints leading to the pill box might be visible, but the tide had been and gone removing any traces there might have been. Stone had to make a decision whether to continue or call the search off – not easy.

"How long will it take to get some dogs down here Inspector?"

"I should think ten minutes maximum."

"Okay, but tell them to approach from the shore. We've already muddled the scent on the track we came down, let's not make it worse."

Nearer fifteen minutes later two Springer spaniels with their handler appeared from the water's edge. The handler directed the dogs to the makeshift bed, they frantically sniffed around, their tails wagging furiously then they were led outside. Stone was bemused, the dogs just stood there sniffing the air for a moment or two and then they were off, not up the track but along the waterfront, there was no way she could keep up with them and their handler, she would rely on the radio.

After five or six minutes the handler radioed in to say the dogs had lost the scent, he'd come to a water filled dyke with a wooden plank across to a field of sugar beet and there was no indication which way the suspect had fled.

Stone had never quite known what to believe about Gallagher/Gilligan from his file, but if he was a soldier he had obviously been highly trained in evasion and survival, to her that could mean one thing – special forces; not her world at all. But, they didn't know that it was him they were chasing - it could just be some tramp.

Strange she thought - no answer from her boss' mobile. She'd walked away from the pill box to make her call. On calling the main line at Thames House she was told he had just undergone an operation for a burst ulcer, it was thought he was going to be okay but was still in recovery. The decision had to be all hers.

"Okay Inspector let's call it off. I'm very sorry but it looks like we're chasing shadows. I'll get a general alert put out for him and we'll keep an eye on his place in Scotland but I don't hold out much hope. Thank you and all your officers for their help."

"Okay Miss, I'll get everyone to stand down. It's a shame we'll never know if he was here or not. I'll give you a lift back to the guest house – do you mind if we go via the road blocks?"

Short, balding, half-moon glasses, corpulent and wearing a sober dark blue suit and tie – how would she describe him Stone was thinking. Ordinary, a man she thought that didn't smile very much – probably very boring too.

"Good morning everyone, thank you for coming in at this early hour, my name is Desmond Hillyard."

The meeting was at Thames House; it was 7am on a rainy morning. Maria Webley, Simmonds' secretary, McLeod and Boswell were also present. After the introductions Hillyard started by saying.

"I have been tasked by the Prime Minister to take over the running of MI5 from Max Simmonds while he's in hospital. Before I go any further, to those that don't know he is expected to make a full recovery, but he does need a rest – he won't be back for at least three weeks. No visit's allowed for the moment. I have been briefed by the PM and Mrs Webley has filled in some of the gaps, it would be helpful you could all do the same.

"There are a number of pressing issues that need to be dealt with apart from the day-to-day running of the service but, first of all, I would like to address the recent attempt on our future King's life. Miss Stone, I know that you won't have had time to file your report on your visit to Lincolnshire so perhaps you could tell us how you got on."

"Yes sir. Extensive searches were made in two areas near the Wash; house to house enquiries were carried out too. The only thing found was evidence that someone had recently slept in a disused military building near the water. Dogs were called in and they picked up a scent but lost it after a short distance. In the absence of any sightings or reports of anything unusual I tried to contact Mr Simmonds. He wasn't answering his mobile so I rang the main switchboard and was informed that he was in hospital; after due consideration I decided to call the search off."

"Did you have the authority to do that?"

"Yes, given by Mr Simmonds before I went."

"I see. There was a line of thought that one of the terrorists had escaped capture and swum to the shore. This was conjecture I believe?"

"Yes it was but, it was possible – the Wash has been swum before."

"Okay. Having failed to find the suspect do you believe he did make it to the shore and is still at large?"

Stone thought before she answered.

"The evidence says no but, my gut instinct says yes. I'm sorry if I seem pedantic sir."

"That's alright, you're being honest. What are you proposing we do about your gut instinct?"

She felt intimidated by the way she was being questioned; perhaps it was just his manner.

"I have issued a general alert, we have good images of the man, and I have asked Police Scotland to keep an eye on his cottage in Argyll, in case he should turn up there, sir."

"That all seems very thorough Miss Stone, thank you very much. It's now nearly seventy two hours since the assassination attempt and we've had a press embargo in place since then. The Duke hasn't been seen and they are pushing the Palace for information about him. No-one has claimed responsibility for the shooting because we haven't announced that it succeeded. This leaves us with a dilemma. If we announce the attempt was a failure, we will never know who was behind it. If we say he's dead the media will crucify us, the public outrage will be enormous, but a group will claim they did it. The other thing is who tipped us off? That's just as important."

He sat back in his chair and looked around the room, searching for an answer. Boswell and McLeod had never heard of this Hillyard, yes, they had been informed of his appointment by the Prime Minister but they were both wary.

McLeod spoke first. "I've given both questions a lot of thought. The only whisper we've had is a rumour the Sheikh or Sultan is high up in the Muslim Brotherhood. Many of us believe that ISIL is the military wing of The Brotherhood. I would gamble that if they thought the Duke was dead they would claim they did it.

"As for the informant it can only be one of two people. Paradoxically, it's either Gallagher or the Sheikh. The former is supposed to have been deep undercover working against the IRA when he was with the Ulster Constabulary - if this is true he has the skills needed."

"I'm sorry to interrupt but why do you say, supposed to have been deep undercover? Where did that information come from?" asked Hillyard.

"Most of his file and his records are a complete fabrication and only utilise information that is available to the government. The Sheikh is far more complex – I think he works for the Egyptian intelligence services, it was they that got him released but, try as I might, I cannot get conformation of this." The tip off came through one of our own servers, so one of them must be able to penetrate our systems, not an easy task."

There was a long pause before Hillyard spoke again.

"Do you have any thoughts Commander Boswell?"

"I can only agree with Betine, sorry, Mrs McLeod, what she says makes sense. But, whoever it is has to have a controller and someone must know who that is. We've discussed this possibility before but that person is unknown to us."

"And you Miss Stone - do have any comments?"

"I've no working knowledge of the Sheikh so I cannot comment. However, I have got to know Gallagher's way of thinking pretty well and I think he's a distinct possibility."

Another pause, Hillyard sat there with his hands forming a steeple, deep in thought.

"What I'm going to recommend to the PM provided no-one has other ideas is the following. There has been an unsuccessful attempt on the Duke of Cambridge's life at his country residence Anmer Hall. He and his family are unharmed and are in good health. The attack had all the hallmarks of so called ISIL and was foiled by an informant. The assailants lost their lives while being pursued across the Wash in East Anglia."

"Sir, what about Hammond? If the press got hold of him and he starts talking, he could expose Gallagher and the Sheikh. If they are working with us this could jeopardise them," said Stone.

"A very good point Miss Stone, we must make sure that Hammond is left out of this altogether. I believe he is going to be released without charge; a gentle reminder might be needed to ensure he never talks to the press. I believe the RAF and the RNLI can be relied upon to say nothing.

"Well I think we have solved the dilemma, thank you all. If so called ISIL are involved they'll be pretty fed up to learn of an informant, we'll see if they have anything to say."

Stone felt that she might have underestimated this boring little man.

Chapter

32

Simmonds had fallen behind the curve due to his operation. Kindly Stone had got the main newspapers delivered to his room in the clinic enabling him to catch up when he came to. He was pleased to read of the nation's gratitude for the Duke's life and that he and his family were all well. Equally pleasing was the praise for the security services – a rare plaudit.

Fed up with being confined to the clinic and, against all advice, he discharged himself. He went to his house in Regent's Park and a nurse attended three times a day, he thought she was as ugly as sin otherwise he might have had some fun - he disposed of her services after two days.

He took the train to Cornwall for a long weekend with his wife and son; they would spend the summer there. He came to a decision while lying on the beach, he was going to retire. Being head of MI5 was stressful and his doctor had told him in no uncertain terms that if he carried on exposed to that level of stress he would be dead in two years. He'd been doing the job for six years and this ulcer business was clearly a warning, besides he was getting bored. He was 55 years old and was in no need of employment, he had a great final salary pension, a number of inherited shares and a healthy sum in the bank. He had friends in high places all over the world and it would be good to see them out of the work context – it was time to enjoy ones self.

When he returned to London he started going into the office for an hour or two at a time to get acclimatised, it was a busy as ever. He was just leaving Thames House on one such day when he bumped into Stone in the foyer - she asked how he was and when she might be able to speak to him.

"I'm fine thank you but just going home now for a nap. Why don't you come over later and we can sit in the garden on this lovely day and have a chat? Shall we say 6pm?"

She hesitated for a moment.

"Yes sir, I'd love to. Where do I go?"

He gave her the address and directions. She had no idea where he lived or what to expect, she didn't know why but she was excited.

The charming white painted cottage with Gothic windows, a slate roof and roses over the doorway was set back from one of the entrances to Regent's Park, it sat behind black iron railings that matched the gates to the park.

Just as she was about to ring the door bell the black painted door swung open, Simmonds was wearing shorts and an open neck shirt.

"Ah, well done Nat you made it, come through to the garden."

She followed him through the entrance hall then a sitting room to the French doors leading on to a terrace. An iron and glass table with matching chairs sat under a vine covered pergola, the scents from the many flowers and the vine was divine.

"Now, before we start Nat, two things. One, when we are not in the office please call me Max. Two, and most importantly, what would you like to drink? I'm going to have a cold beer but there are most things."

"I'll join you with a beer sir, oops sorry Max."

He disappeared inside giving her the opportunity to look around the L shaped garden. Enclosed on the two sides with a very tall hedge, she thought it might be Yew, it was peaceful - you wouldn't know you were in a very busy part of London. The garden wasn't very big but it was expertly planted and cared for, she wondered if Simmonds did that himself, she asked him when he returned with drinks and some nibbles. He laughed and said no, he paid one of the park gardeners – a good arrangement.

"Now, what did you want to ask me?"

"I cannot stop thinking about Gallagher and the Sultan; I eat them, drink them and sleep them and my head is full of questions I'm afraid. I hope that I'm not being impertinent in asking you, as head of MI5, if you would automatically know if someone in the organisation was working undercover, someone like Gilligan for example?"

"Well, that was during my predecessor's time so I can't answer for him, but the answer is no, not by any means. The security services in this country are compartmentalised and with a degree of autonomy, no-one, with one exception, knows all of what's going on, that exception is the PM. You're not being impertinent by the way. How's the beer?"

"The beer is delicious thank you. There have been suggestions that the Sultan may be working for us, but what I don't understand is if the plan originated with the Muslim Brotherhood of which he's supposed to be a prominent member why would he sabotage it?"

"Do you play chess Nat?"

"No."

"Then I suggest you learn, you'll find it helps with reasoning and with being one step ahead. My thoughts are that the Sultan heard of the plan first hand and it made sense for him to take it on and control it, given his position he wouldn't attract suspicion."

"But he wouldn't be able to do it himself would he?"

"No, I don't think so but have you considered that he and Gallagher might have been working together?"

"Blimey, no I hadn't. What would happen to the Sultan if the Brotherhood found out?"

"I should think they'd execute him, if they haven't done so already."

There was a pause in the conversation. House martins and swallows were busy hawking for their insect dinner, it was just after 7pm and it was that quiet it was easy to imagine you were in the depths of the countryside. She was offered another beer and accepted, she wasn't over the limit and she was catching a cab home anyway.

Simmonds came back with the beers and sat down.

"I'm wondering if there is a connection between the attack on the Duke and the attack on Glasgow airport, Gallagher/Gilligan's hair was found at both. Okay, I know they weren't a conclusive match but they were close, and both attacks failed. And, the other thing is the photograph of the Sultan and Gilligan at the embassy function in Kabul."

Another pause, Simmonds was thinking.

"You know I think you've cracked it Nat, well done, and you don't even play chess!"

They both laughed, she was so pleased with herself.

"Sadly I don' think we'll ever know Nat, they're probably both dead."

"Changing the subject Max, is that a yew hedge?"

"Yes it is, it's magnificent; it was planted when the lodge was built in 1820, so that makes it what – nearly two hundred years old."

Just then out of nowhere a breeze got up, slightly chilled Stone involuntarily shuddered, she was wearing her habitual T shirt and designer cut jeans but no coat.

"Come on let's go inside, I've made a Greek salad if you'd like to share it with me."

He was standing behind her with a hand on each of her shoulders, the contact made her tingle. It all seemed so natural, not contrived as her right arm went up to his left hand and touched it without thinking. He bowed his head and kissed her lightly on the forehead, she turned and with eyes wide open kissed him fully on the mouth – her head was spinning.

She was thinking this is dangerous, but dismissed the thought immediately.

He was thinking, bugger the pay roll, I'm retiring.

Chapter
33

Over the last two weeks Stone and Simmonds had seen each other on a number of occasions, they couldn't get enough of each other; both were certain their affair was secret which made it much more exciting.

Simmonds had come to an agreement over his retirement - it was to be the 31st December when he would hand over to Desmond Hillyard until a full time replacement was found. He felt an enormous weight lift from his shoulders; he hadn't told Stone but would do so when they met in the evening.

For the past fortnight Stone had been away from Thames House on two courses, counter terrorism and firearms, she enjoyed them both although she wasn't too keen on guns. She was seriously happy in her relationship with Max - she'd never had a lover quite like him; handsome, well endowed, interesting and attentive like many older men.

They'd settled into a routine. Always meeting at his lodge, as he called it, he would prepare their meal, he loved to cook; they never went out. After they would listen to music and he would teach her to play chess, she learned quickly and before too long nearly beat him on two successive occasions – he was right, it did make her think more laterally. Then they would go to bed and make passionate love all night long.

She was enchanted by his home - it seemed a little run down inside but that was its charm. Some of the rugs had holes in them and the silk curtains were threadbare, but the gilded picture frames and mirrors combined with the soft lighting gave it the feeling of a decadent Bohemian love nest.

"I've got two surprises for you Nat,"

They were in the middle of dinner – lamb cutlets.

"Goodie, I love surprises."

"Well.................." He was dragging it out on purpose.

"Oh get on, don't tease me!"

They laughed.

"Well.......the first one is I'm retiring at the end of December."

"That is wonderful news. Have you thought about what you might do when you have time on your hands?"

"Yes I have. When I'm not in bed with you I thought I might do some travelling to see the many friends I have around the world."

"How can you be in bed with me if you're on the other side of the world?"

"Ah, I've been thinking about that, perhaps you might like to come with me sometimes - what do you think?"

"That sounds wonderful but I'm not going to give up my career, I love it too much."

"I would hope not, let's just cross each bridge as we get to it. Now, the other surprise - what are you doing on Saturday?"

"I'm going to be in Norfolk staying with my cousin for the weekend – why?"

"Perfect. You've been invited to an informal lunch at Anmer Hall by the Duke and Duchess of Cambridge."

"Wow, that's amazing – so exciting. Why?"

"They want to thank you for your assistance in helping to foil the plot against the Duke. I'm going with McLeod and Boswell and I believe the PM will be there."

She left work early on Friday to go to Norfolk; it was a lovely warm afternoon as she wheeled the bike out of the lock-up. She felt pretty hot in her leathers but started to cool off once underway. Traffic was heavy and she was in a hurry because she was so thrilled about lunch tomorrow, she'd made no mention of it to Fiona and couldn't wait to tell her.

Unable to sleep that night because of nerves she went and sat in the garden, it was a hot night, she was naked. So much had happened in the last few months she reflected, her life had changed completely. Max's proposals sounded wonderful, but she must keep her feet on the ground and progress in her work – who knows where that will lead she asked herself.

She arrived at Anmer on the dot. After waiting for the gate to open she went slowly up the winding drive, at the end a man, probably a footman, was waiting to direct her to where to park her bike, there were several official looking cars there.

She felt self-conscious in her bright green leathers as she followed the footman along the side of the building to the rear, as she turned the corner onto the terrace the Duke and Duchess were waiting, broad grins on their faces. Fiona had told her she should curtsy when she met them; she tried but almost fell over.

The Duchess laughed and said, "Nat, we don't do that here, I'm Kate, welcome to Anmer," she extended her hand, "and this is William," he did the same, they all shook hands.

She was blushing but beginning to feel at ease. "I'm very pleased to meet you both. Is there somewhere I can get out of these leathers please, I'm boiling?"

"They're wonderful, I love the colour. Of course, if you go into the door there and then the second on the left you'll find a cloakroom - join us by the pool when you're ready," said Kate.

Wearing bright yellow tailored trousers and a purple silk shirt she looked stunning as she joined the company by the enormous pool. It was difficult for her and Max as they wanted to kiss each other but couldn't, she was saying hello to McLeod and Boswell when Kate asked what she would like to drink – she chose a cold cordial, too hot for alcohol.

She was thinking how strange it was to be at the very spot where the failed attempt to kill her host took place so recently.

William, wearing a badly patched single piece striped swimsuit, announced that the pool was there to use not look at, it needed Christening as he put it. "There are plenty of costumes and towels in the dressing rooms, please help yourselves"

Nobody hung around, it was hot and the pool looked so inviting. Once changed everyone, apart from William, jumped in just as the clattering of a helicopter landing interrupted – it was the PM. William remained on the terrace tending the BBQ while the PM changed and joined everyone in the pool.

Stone and Kate were sitting in loungers on the terrace; the others were still in the pool. They were getting on like a house on fire – Kate was fascinated by the motorbike and confessed to always wanting one but William wasn't to keen on the idea.

He'd just got out of the pool to check on the BBQ when Stone could hear footsteps approaching from behind – another guest. William walked past her to greet the visitor.

"Ah Jamie, you made it well done, it's great to see you."

"It's good to see you too Wills."

"Come over and let me introduce you to people."

The visitor stopped to kiss Kate and then turned to Stone with his hand extended.

"Nat, this is Jamie Grant, we served together when I was flying down in the Falklands. Jamie, this is Nat Stone."

Her hand went out automatically, but her mouth and eyes were wide open in shock, it was Gallagher! A strange thought went through her head – have I just shaken the hand of a dead man?

The end

About the Author

John Vost was born on Epping, Essex in 1945. He has lived in London, Paris, Moscow and is at present in Norfolk.

A fine art valuer and advisor for more than forty years he discovered a love of writing in 2011. Since then he has written four other novels and a text book on clocks, currently he is working on a children's book about dogs inspired by his own Jack Russell terrier Jack.

Books by the same author

The Visitor's Book

Based on true events this is a chilling story of life in Moscow, just after the collapse of the Soviet Union, and the present in the UK. The story revolves around Hitler's own guest book retrieved from the ruins of Berlin by the Russians at the end of World War 11. The book is tracked down by neo-Nazis and other undesirables to England where it becomes the subject of a bloody tug o' war culminating in a violent showdown in sleepy Norfolk.

Saviour of the World

Set in the beautiful Channel Islands and Derbyshire with a hint of romance this is a tale about an Old Master painting salvaged from the bottom of the sea and then stolen. The trail to recover it uncovers a smuggling ring, drugs and murder ending in a siege in a remote cottage in the Peak District where police officers are killed.

The Letter

This story, again revolving around a stolen painting this time an impressionist, is set mostly in the stunning landscapes of the west Highlands of Scotland. By Renoir, the painting goes missing from a Baronial mansion in Lochaber, the police and insurers are incompetent and through frustration the owner assembles a team to track the painting down. The trail leads them to Tangiers and to the Fens in Lincolnshire and goes full circle to discovery.

Murder in the Gorge

A thriller inspired by the brutal killing of a British/Iraqi family in the French Alps in 2012. The investigation by DCI Jamie Phillips uncovers nuclear secrets and a spy ring in the British establishment is set in London and the beautiful Lozere region of France. It's his misfortune he becomes infatuated with a beautiful woman but he can't decide who's side she's on.

#0018 - 300816 - C0 - 210/148/11 - PB - DID1564477